The Storm Tower

By
Dan McGrath

DanMcGrath.net

The Storm Tower
Copyright © 2022 Dan McGrath

This book relates an entirely fictional story. Any similarities to real events or people living or dead is strictly coincidence.

PAPERBACK

FIRST EDITION

Published by Dan McGrath
DanMcGrath.net

Cover Art by Dan McGrath

ISBN: 9798351946290

Contents

Chapter One: A Dark and Stormy Morning   1
Chapter Two: A Black Tale   13
Chapter Three: Death in the Dark   18
Chapter Four: Visitors in the Night   26
Chapter Five: Bumps in the Shadows   33
Chapter Six: The Fog of Time   40
Chapter Seven: What Lies Beneath   45
Chapter Eight: The Shadow on the High Walk   51
Chapter Nine: Brotherhood   61
Chapter Ten: Whispers   65
Chapter Eleven: The Length of Nights   74
Chapter Twelve: A Prince, Named   78
Chapter Thirteen: Dark Deeds   82
Chapter Fourteen: Into the Dark   85
Chapter Fifteen: Within the Glow   96
Chapter Sixteen: A Dark Hand of Magic   100
Chapter Seventeen: Bother   107
Chapter Eighteen: Knock, Knock   112
Chapter Nineteen: Of Wind and Stardust   116
Chapter Twenty: Fury at the Gates   128

Chapter Twenty-One: The Wind Makers   137
Chapter Twenty-Two: The Tower, Cracked   142
Chapter Twenty-Three: A Plan   147
Chapter Twenty-Four: Reg   153
Chapter Twenty-Five: Raleigh   156
Chapter Twenty-Six: Inga   158
Chapter Twenty-Seven: The Wrath of Ranius   161
Epilogue   166
Appendix I: Diagrams   169
Spoiler Warning   171
Appendix II: Cast of Characters   172
Appendix III: From the Tomes   178

Dedicated with thanks to:

Brandon Gustafson

Donovan Ewer

Jeff Wolske

Robert Fahy

Jessica McGrath

Todd Williams

Richard Bradbury

Cris Croissant

Patrick Williams

Dan Williams

Thea Bradbury

Amy Bradbury

John Ewaldt

Kathy McGrath, my dear, departed mother who first read to me,
The Hobbit and started me off in my enduring love of fantasy
books.

A Dark and Stormy Morning

There was a dim yellow light in the sky. The rains and mists obscured it now, but it had appeared in the dark enough times that Raleigh was sure he'd really seen it.

"There's definitely something there," Raleigh called back over his shoulder, tightening his hood against the harsh elements.

Wind and icy rain lashed him and his companion where they stood upon a stony ledge.

"It would be safer to wait until morning to seek its source," Lana called back, grimacing against the soaking chill. "I'm going back to the shelter!"

Raleigh laughed humorlessly. "There's no safety here, my lady!" Still, he followed the black-robed young woman back down a slick incline, taking a glass sphere the size of a walnut from his pouch. It produced light. Not remotely adequate light for the conditions, but better than nothing.

Lightning was rather more effectively clarifying their surroundings, and with alarming frequency.

If there had been any vegetation, the higher ground might have made a modestly better camp site, but Raleigh's particular magic could only work with the foliage closer to the brush.

The tiny shelter he'd conjured was a watertight dome comprised of sticks, mud and leaves, low to the ground and easily missed by one not looking for it.

As they approached, an opening appeared – slick, muddy vegetation parting of its own accord. They crawled inside the close space. There was barely room to sit fully upright, with their heads just touching the thankfully dry ceiling of the dome. A blanket of matted dry leaves and foliage also formed the floor. Raleigh's little sphere lit the interior well.

They struggled out of their soaking outer cloaks – hers black and his a rusty maroon color.

"I'd be grateful for a fire to dry off by, if only it wouldn't kill us in here," Raleigh said, "but I'm afraid we'll be wishing for even this level of comfort in a few hours or so. This spell isn't going to hold up much longer."

Lana shrugged. She'd not yet mastered the shelter spell herself. Her companions used to manage that. "We could be dead."

Raleigh nodded somberly. "Right. Let's try to sleep a little before we're homeless."

"Or until…"

Raleigh nodded again, then laid down, curled on his side. Lana nuzzled into him and, curled up together to share some scant warmth, they fell asleep quickly, exhausted.

The sounds of blasting winds and thunder crashing about the tiny leaf hut didn't much disturb their slumber, but they did receive a rude awakening when, as Raleigh had predicted, their shelter disintegrated in the wee hours before dawn.

Shocked awake by a deluge falling from the flashing sky, Raleigh and Lana hastened back into their still wet cloaks, for all the good they were.

"Those lights you saw," Lana said, "You're certain that's the tower?"

"Not certain, but I don't know what else it might be. If I'm right, we should be able to shelter there. We'd best be on with it. No sense in standing still, now."

"How's your strength?" Lana asked.

"I don't feel replenished, if that's what you mean. There's power in that direction, though. Can you sense it?"

Lana closed her eyes, concentrating. In her mind's eye, she could see colorful, wispy and wavering ribbons of light. They were force lines or "mana" as some said. Fuel for magic.

"There's a lot of it." Lana perked up a bit.

"There's a canyon to the south of here. If we can find a good way through these hills we should be able to follow the canyon to the tower," Raleigh said.

"About how far do you think?" Lana stretched a hand towards the magic energy, but she couldn't quite seem to attract it.

"Less than a day, I'd guess – but with these conditions…"

"Right. Let's be on with it. I'd rather not dwell on the alternatives." Lana found enough energy in the air to produce a little heat. Her hands flickered with a faint light, like ghostly flames. She could feel the heat near her body without it burning.

Raleigh had his own spells to use against the elements, but he'd exhausted his reserves summoning shelter and hadn't yet had adequate rest. He tightened his hood further against the punishing rains so only his eyes were visible and the two pressed on into the dark and stormy morning.

"I'm so hungry. I keep thinking of the inn near my family's estate and the keeper there cooking me up a sizzling, juicy cut of steak. With cauliflower and heaps of butter. Hell, just the cauliflower could make my mouth water about now," Lana said as they trudged on, "but I guess I won't die of thirst." She raised her hands towards the dark and pouring sky.

Raleigh glanced at her. rainwater was cascading off her nose. "Well, at least I'd be none the wiser if my lady was drooling," he said, but there didn't seem to be much humor left in him just then.

The light sphere Raleigh carried only lit a few paces before them in the mist and pounding rain. If it was day or night, they couldn't have seen much difference, but frequent lightning helped them roughly keep their bearing. After a while, it also painted the distinct shape of a high tower in silhouette against the electrified sky.

They'd found the canyon and followed its ridge westward for miles. It was slow going and treacherous, but eventually, the ground evened out and opened up before them. Another series of lightning flashes revealed the shape of an arched bridge to the south-west.

"Ah!" Raleigh grew excited. "There should be a road ahead. We're close."

Raleigh seemed to know at least a little about this mysterious tower and its environs. He was a few years older and more advanced in magecraft. Lana was grateful for that. When she'd found herself trapped, her escape route impassable, she'd felt nearly hopeless and then, suddenly, there was Raleigh Talanth.

They did indeed come upon a road. It was paved with flagstones that finally kept their boots out of the sucking mud. The road curved to the south and brought them to a chasm where the earth had given out. An arched stone bridge spanned it and beyond, the road continued onto a natural causeway jutting into the deep canyon. On a butte at the end of the causeway stood the imposing tower, the dark canyon, here bent like a horseshoe, engulfing the land around it. Yellowish lights shimmered from the tower's high windows.

"The Painted Tower," Raleigh introduced with a gesture.

The dark edifice didn't look very colorful to Lana. In the storm, it may as well have been "painted" black, but she wasn't going to quarrel.

The appearance of shelter so near quickened their pace through the deluge.

Lana was surprised when the massive metal door drew slowly open as they neared the structure. It didn't seem to faze Raleigh.

Flickering firelight from within promised reprieve.

Casting aside doubt or caution, Lana almost sprinted, eager to be sheltered from the vile storm that had plagued her existence for days.

Raleigh jogged to keep up with her.

Beyond the massive entry, they stood dripping in the foyer, taking in their surroundings. The door closed with a scrape and a thud behind the soaking pair as a puddle formed beneath them. Ahead, there was a blazing hearth. Glass lanterns also illuminated the entry.

No one immediately greeted them, but Raleigh spied pegs set in the wall. Two maroon-colored cloaks hung there. Raleigh hung up his own sopping cloak and there were three. Lana added her black, hooded cloak and they moved in closer to the fire.

"I've never been more grateful for flame than at this moment," said Lana.

Raleigh nodded absently, looking all around. Wood-paneled walls near the entry formed a short corridor that opened into the rectangular room. Around the corners, closed wooden doors were framed into wooden walls. The rest of the perimeter was stone.

From outside in the storm, the rain-slick tower appeared black, but now they could see that it was built from the same stratified stone of the surrounding canyon and it was mostly a dark reddish color with bands of ochre here and there and spots of black and brown. From inside, it did seem a bit like the local geology had painted the tower with some abstract geometry. There was an uncommon beauty to it.

There was a simple padded divan and there were a couple elegantly crafted wooden chairs. Runes were carved into some of the stones up by the high ceiling of the room.

A larger stone-arched doorway with the door ajar was set in a corner of the room. Stone steps were visible beyond.

Raleigh turned his attention to the wall carvings near the ceiling. Something up there had caught his eye. Movement, or a flicker of light, maybe.

"Some storm," said a voice from the steps.

Raleigh and Lana spun around.

A young man in red robes stood in the archway. "You are welcome to shelter here. I'll find you some dry clothes and something hot to eat. My name is Reg. Reginald Partha, but please just call me Reg."

Now, Raleigh did seem somewhat surprised. "Thank you, Lord Partha... Reg. I'm Raleigh Talanth and my companion here is the lady Lana Arcana."

Reg provided them everything promised, and more. Beds with linens on soft mattresses were made ready and a flagon of mulled wine produced.

"You must be made comfortable and rested before we hear your tale," Reg commented.

"I'm grateful for that," Lana said.

"Who's we?" Raleigh inquired.

"There are only the three of us in the tower," Reg answered. "Myself and Lords Davis and Vardan Talanth."

Raleigh nodded with a satisfied and knowing look. "Ah" was all he said to that.

"It makes sense now, does it?" Lana asked after Reg had left them. The tower was situated roughly at the far border of lands long controlled by the Talanths. Beyond were dangerous wildlands — the sort of area that attracted young bands of adventuring magi – like Lana. "You weren't expecting to be met by a Partha in here."

They rested a few hours in the small room that had been provided, but awoke to the tantalizing aroma of meat cooking over a fire.

The manaflows that converged in the tower's environs had a strong rejuvenating effect on the two.

Lana rose from the bed. She was dressed in a slightly too-big red silk top and cream-colored leggings that Reg had provided. Out of her heavy black robes and drenched outer cloak, Raleigh saw for the first time that she was a small young lady. Thin and petite. Clean, dry and slightly rested, her longish blonde hair framed a youthful face. She was pretty when she didn't look like someone had tried to drown a black cat.

Being that the tower was a Talanth holding, there was no shortage of clean and dry maroon robes for Raleigh, so he was dressed, as usual, in his clan color. He had wavy, shoulder-length brown hair and bright, hazel eyes.

It was the first time they'd really seen what each other looked like.

Lana's stomach was growling audibly. "Whatever that smell is, I need it," she said.

"Something better than cauliflower, I'd bet."

They weren't immediately sure where to go. Reg had led them through the arched doorway into a smaller, round auxiliary tower that seemed to serve primarily as the stairway for the square main tower, but contained small semi-circular rooms on a couple levels. The stone steps spiraled into darkness around the perimeter with occasional landings on the various levels of the square tower. They'd earlier gone up past three landings to get to their bedroom.

They followed the smell downward to the second level and there, found two of their hosts seated at a table. Though the tower appeared enormous from outside, the rooms within were small and the space that seemed to serve as both kitchen and dining room was close.

"I know all the stories about this old tower," a bearded man with dark brown hair was saying. "We might not be as safe here as you believe."

"People who died... Carelessness was their undoing. This old tower has stood longer than you and I and it'll be here, standing strong, holding and watching these lands long after we're dead," said a plump, older man in a rusty-colored, embroidered vest.

"I'd prefer if that was still a long time into the future. These storms are the worst I've seen and the portal..."

"Excuse us," said Raleigh. "I hate to interrupt, but I'd not want to be the sort of guest thought to eavesdrop on his hosts, either."

The older man stood, setting his knife down on a platter. "Ah. You're looking lively. I'm Davis and this here is My nephew Vardan. Might be he's an uncle of yours, or some such."

The bearded man nodded. He wore the maroon robes of Clan Talanth and Raleigh noticed an ornate golden amulet on a chain around his neck. From its aura, Raleigh could instantly tell that it was imbued with a powerful magic.

"I think we're cousins, actually. A generation removed, if I have the right Vardan," Raleigh said. "I'm Raleigh Talanth and my companion is Lady Lana Arcana."

"I know who you are," said the gray-haired old man. "Got caught in the storm, seeking shelter, and so on."

"Indeed and we're most grateful."

"Oh, yes. We very much are," Lana said enthusiastically.

Reg hollered distantly from up the stair. "There's a light on the water! Might be we're going to have some more company!"

"Go take a look and see what he's on about," Davis said.

Vardan got up from the small table and left the room.

"I don't imagine there are many people about, but with this storm, whoever is around would seek shelter here if they can find the place," Raleigh observed. "What was it you were saying about a portal?"

"Nothing. I mean, I wasn't. Vardan was just being a bit jittery over the weather. Nothing to worry about," Davis assured.

Raleigh didn't pry further.

The elder Talanth picked up two earthenware cups from a shelf and filled them from a kettle. "Good warm wine," he said, setting them down for his guests. Help yourself to a cut of meat." He pointed to a leg of some beast that was roasting over a low flame in the hearth and sat back down to his own meal.

After they'd finished their breakfast, Vardan stuck his head back into the small kitchen. "There's definitely a light bobbing around down there. Some sort of river vessel that's heading right into trouble," he said. "There's magic about it, though."

"Well, you're probably right that they won't be able to get much further than the bend, so more company's about certain, I suppose," Davis replied.

"I've never seen so much activity here in my life," said Vardan. "Reg said something about the perimeter runes glinting, too, so I'm heading downstairs to look around and I might as well take a peek at the portal, just in case."

Davis furrowed his brow. "No reason to think…" Then he nodded. "Ah, I'll be down for a look myself in a moment," he said.

Vardan disappeared into the stairway.

"About this portal," Raleigh started.

"Aye, it's of the magic sort, if that's what you're asking," Davis provided with a slight air of annoyed reluctance.

"I'd like to see this magic boat," Lana said.

Davis stood up. "Probably not much to see," he said, "but the lookout's at the top of the stairs, of course." He turned to Raleigh. "Well, You're some kind of kin, I reckon, so, why not, my boy? Why don't you come with me then, and I'll show you the portal you're so curious about."

Raleigh rose from his seat and followed Davis down the stone steps while Lana ascended to the top of the tower.

The main stairs wound around the perimeter of a silo-shaped second tower attached to a corner of the main square tower keep. At the base of that round stair tower was a heavy-looking iron hatch. It was warded with protective glyphs that faintly glowed. That hatch led to the undercroft. Davis grumbled an incantation and then heaved it open. A narrower stair spiraled down into darkness. Another incantation produced a faint light that pulsed from somewhere below. Raleigh followed Davis down.

Deep in the heart of the butte upon which the tower stood, they came into a circular chamber. At its center was a column of polished white stone. From that column radiated three stone arches, equidistant, like spokes. The arches each appeared to be carved from a single piece of sparkling white stone.

Raleigh recognized that the symbols carved into the arches were some sort of magical writings, but they weren't entirely familiar.

"Don't pass under any of those arches," Davis warned. Those are portals to the three realms. The fabric between is weak, here, but this structure holds it together. Those portals enable passage – for us, anyway."

"The three realms of the sky, land and sea? You just… walk through?"

"Or wind, earth and water. And it's not *quite* as simple as that. You have to have deliberate intent to enter the other realm and it only works for a true mage, but still, steer clear."

"And what of the fourth realm?"

Davis shook his head. "That realm is far from here."

"Surely it's everywhere," Raleigh said.

"Elemental fire is everywhere, aye. All the realms overlap, but the border between the realm of fire and our own is wide, here. It's nothing to do with the local convergence. The fabric *here* is weak between our world and the three realms."

"I see."

"Well, I don't see anything to fret about down here, but say, I thought Vardan was coming down to look himself..."

"Must have gotten diverted," Raleigh said. "I don't recognize those glyphs." he pointed to the writing on one of the arches.

"Well, that's very old magic. Very old, indeed. Predates the Empire, ya see?"

Raleigh's interest was rising rapidly. "Which Empire and by what reckoning? I wonder... I have learned a thing or two about this tower," he gushed. "The history is muddled. Much of it disagrees, but I have suspected that it's older than the official story lets on."

Davis cracked a small smile. The first hint of such an expression Raleigh had seen on the old man since meeting him.

Raleigh turned his attention to a carving in the wall opposite the stairs. It was shaped like an archway and was similar in style to the glittering white arches that marked the elemental portals. The whole thing was sheer stone and didn't appear to be a functioning egress, however. "What's this?"

Davis shrugged. "Magic door? Might lead to a cave by here, best we've been able to guess, but nobody's been able to figure it out. Its secret has been lost to time."

Raleigh studied this other magic door for a moment. It was carved right into the reddish stone of the wall. Raleigh noticed then that while the tower was built of quarried blocks, the undercroft was dug right into the natural stone. There were no seams or joins on the smooth, curved walls.

"Where did Vardan get off to?" Davis turned to the stairs, then back to Raleigh. "This is something of a family secret, you understand?" He gestured for Raleigh to come along.

Not very closely guarded. "Of course." Raleigh buttoned his lip, then, with a small sigh, followed the elder Talanth back up the steps.

A Black Tale

Lana found her way to the lookout. Luminescent spheres lit the room, but not so much as the dazzling flashes of lightning that continued unabated outside.

There were three metal doors and twelve great windows, fitted with thick, but smooth and crystal-clear glass all around. There was the door she stepped through from the round tower and the other two appeared to lead out onto the square tower's high parapet walks.

Peering out a window, Lana could vaguely make out the shape of the canyon far below in contrasted, flickering shadows, but she couldn't see the river or any sign of a light that might be on the water.

The room was surprisingly quiet, considering the storm that was battering the tower. She could barely hear the thunder, let alone the rain or wind. There was an odd humming tone that seemed to emanate from above, in the round tower stair, however. It was almost musical, but monotonous.

Lana turned her attention back to the stairs. Although the lookout was the upper-most floor of the square tower, more stairs wound a little farther up the perimeter of the round tower. She followed them up a to a smaller, but slightly higher turret and belfry. The light within was dim. Reg, the scarlet-clad young

Partha was peering out a window through a black spyglass with brass fittings.

Like the others below, the windows that looked out in all directions were thick, clear glass. These were glazed in heavy sashes with strongly reinforced iron hinges and unfamiliar mechanisms, presumably to open and allow the sound of the great bell to better ring out of the tower when necessary.

The roof came to a point above, where the bell hung. The storm was louder here and there was an echo throughout the tower. Vibrations from the intense storm were causing the great bell to resonate somewhat – the source of the humming tone Lana had heard.

"Oh, hello," Reg said, noticing Lana. He set his spyglass on a stone ledge. "What's going on below?"

"Vardan said something about going to check on some sort of portal," Lana said.

Concern and curiosity mixed into a frown on the young man's face. "I see."

"Where did you spot this magic boat?" Lana inquired.

"Oh. I've lost sight of it, now, I'm afraid. Can't see its aura anymore, either. It was about there, last I could make it out," he said, pointing out into the stormy dark. "Might be something happened to it. It's damn treacherous out there."

"Don't I know," Lana said.

"Yes. Well, how did you and Lord Raleigh come to require our shelter, if you don't mind my asking?"

Lana looked downward, out a window, into the storm. "I was part of a band," she began, slowly. "My companions and I are – were – out to make ourselves in the wilds. Beyond Talanth, the uncontrolled lands looked especially interesting to us and they were close for us to start our adventures."

"I see. There have been others with the same notion," Reg said. "My father thinks of himself as a modern man and gave me up as a ward and apprentice instead, but I think it's good you're keeping the old ways."

"Ha. The old ways? Maybe not so old. Raleigh and I were just talking about that. He theorizes that the Schism was more recent than the official history says and the way us young magi are tested in the world is actually a newer tradition. He reckons it could have been devised to tame and reclaim all the lands that went wild when the old Empire fell apart."

"My tutor has suggested something similar. Still, it seems a worthy and patriotic endeavor. The adventure."

Lana didn't feel so sure about that. "Patriotic? Sending the young to right the wrongs of our elders? Consider yourself fortunate, here. My friends weren't so lucky. There is nothing romantic about seeing all your friends die."

"Sorry, my lady." Reg cast a glance downward. "Forgive my digression. Please go on."

Lana took a deep breath as she sifted through her recollections. "As we came upon the broken lands, this terrible storm came out of nowhere. It was just absolutely incredible and it all started happening so fast," Lana continued. "There was purple lightning flashing all around and..."

"Purple lightning?"

"Well, yes. And red, too. I think. It was everywhere and wind strong enough to hurl stones. We ran and ran, seeking some cave or crevice for shelter. Flash floods and mud slides turned the earth against us. The way we'd come into the broken lands was even worse – made impassable by a tempest like I've never seen, so we had no choice but to press on toward the wilds. The storm is weaker here, if you can believe it. Back there, it was lethal."

Lana paused and stared distantly for a moment.

The rain, wind and thunder vied to fill the silence. The bell hummed. Reg waited patiently for Lana to resume her tale.

"Daxos D'Normic died first," she said once she'd composed her thoughts. "Something struck his head and almost took it off. He... he..." Lana stopped again to take a deep breath. Tears were welling up. "Well, somehow I found my way to what looked like a passable trail, but the torrential rain made it more treacherous than it looked. I slipped and got washed into a deep, flooded depression. I couldn't climb back out and my magic was exhausted – If I could even think of a spell that would have helped – I'm only a novice, myself.

"I pretty much gave up at that point. Everyone was dead or lost. Dead, I think. I was certain I was next and resigned to it. I was up to my waist in freezing, muddy water, almost wishing it would just be over. And that's where I met Lord Talanth." Lana rubbed at her wet eyes. "He got me out. He seemed to know his way around, somewhat, at least. He got us out of the worst of the storm and he was able to conjure some shelter for us – for a while. When that gave out, he got us here."

Reginald Partha listened intently, hands clasped inside the sleeves of his scarlet robes. "That's a harrowing tale," he said softly. "I'm sorry for your friends. And you."

The small round room flickered from a dizzying barrage of lightning outside. Lana could feel the booming thunderclaps deep in her chest.

Gazing out the window, she said, "It's deadly out there. All of my friends... It was like the storm was alive." Her voice lowered, almost to a whisper. "And malevolent. I feel it now. It wants in."

Reg glanced reflexively into the blackness outside the windows, then changed the subject. "If anyone comes ashore from that vessel, the tower will alert us," he said. "Just like it did when you approached."

"What do you mean?" Lana pulled her gaze from the window to regard Reg.

"There are inscriptions, old runes carved into some of the tower stones – mostly in the great hall, but some in the whisper room that…"

"Whisper room? That's an odd sounding…"

"It's… There's an ancient contrivance in there that allows us to speak with others across the ether. I don't really know much about it. I'm not allowed. Lord Talanth – Lord Davis, that is – he calls it the 'Whisper Room,' but anyway, there are stones in the wall that glow and flash when our perimeters are breached," Reg explained.

"I see. And the Whisper Room is like a messenger spell."

Reg cocked his head and then shook it, slightly. "Not exactly, I don't think. Well, maybe, with similar intent and purpose, I suppose. Like I said, I'm not really allowed in there. Now I'll have to find out what Lord Vardan saw when he went to check the portal."

"Let's do that." Lana agreed, glad to be shedding dark thoughts and darker memories for the nonce.

Death in the Dark

Once back on the ground floor, Davis gestured into the smallish sitting room with the large hearth that the tower residents called the great hall. He briefly pointed out the runes carved into some of the stones in the walls near the ceiling. "These ones mind the grounds," he said, indicating runes on each of the three stone walls in the room. There were similar runes down at the end of the wood-paneled entry hall, above the big front door. "These three mind the portal. If there's a disturbance, lights will chase around in the carvings, so they'll flicker and glow different colors."

"Very ingenious," Raleigh admired the design of the magic, stepping out of the round tower and into the room. What is this one for?"

"Oh, that one means someone wants to talk to us. It hasn't illuminated in decades. These portal runes haven't lit up in my lifetime, for that matter. Now where did blasted Vardan get off to? Excuse me, will you?" Davis ascended the main stair, leaving Raleigh alone to study the runes.

Raleigh recognized most of them, but their styling wasn't common. The runes were old. As old as the tower, probably. How old was that? Before the Schism, for certain. Before the Empire? Which empire was it supposed to predate?

One of the runes flickered red. It was one of the runes that Davis said minded the tower grounds.

Raleigh glanced toward the door and observed just then that the floor was quite wet by the entry. Moving closer, he noticed there were only three cloaks hung by the pegs. Two maroon and one black. One was missing.

Vardan's. *He must have gone outside.*

Raleigh donned his own cloak and opened the door, stepping once again into the hellish wind and rain that raged outside the tower.

He produced his glowing sphere, but still couldn't see much. He made a couple small circuits around the front grounds without spotting any further clues to the whereabouts of his cousin and soon retreated back towards the shelter of the tower. It was punishing and miserable out there.

It felt like it had grown even colder out in the storm, but maybe that was just because Raleigh had become acclimated to the warm, dry comfort of the tower.

The door opened of its own accord as Raleigh approached. Light from inside shone on the ground along with his luminescent sphere and Raleigh spied a glint in the mud. He bent over for a closer look and picked up a golden amulet on a broken chain. Vardan's amulet, he knew. The power he'd sensed in it earlier was no longer present, though.

He stepped through the door and it again secured itself against the wind and rain. Raleigh hung his sopping cloak back on the peg in the wood-paneled entryway.

Now that he was mindful of it, Raleigh could see that there was a damp trail from the front entrance all the way to the arched door that led to the main stair.

"Ah." It looked like Vardan hadn't stayed long outside, either. Raleigh tucked Vardan's dead amulet into a pocket.

One of the runes near the ceiling flickered blue. Raleigh paused and stared at it. He had to double-check his recollection of what Davis had said. It was a portal rune.

Raleigh stepped into the round tower and looked back and forth between the stair and the hatch in the floor.

That magic portal was more interesting than a wet cousin, he decided.

"Let me see," he muttered to himself, as he studied the heavy metal disk in the floor and tried to remember exactly how Davis had opened it. "Grumble grumble mumble bumble... malfermu ci tiun lukon!" he intoned, pushing just a touch of magic energy into the incantation. The hatch opened when he pulled on its thick iron ring.

"Ah ha. Easy," he said to himself, feeling self-satisfied. Down again, he went. Light was still pulsing from below, but it seemed brighter and more erratic.

When he reached the bottom, he could see that the portal was indeed disturbed. Streaks of blue and white light were zooming back and forth, tracing through the carvings on one of the sparkling white arches. And beneath that arch was a shimmer like waves of heat in a desert.

"That's probably not supposed to be doing that," Raleigh said aloud. Not knowing precisely what forces he might be witnessing, and knowing even less on the subject of what to do about it, he decided to make haste back out of the undercroft.

He dashed up the winding stair, resealed the hatch and continued up the tower's main stair. "Lord Davis!" He shouted as he took the steps two a stride. "Davis! Vardan!"

He stopped ascending when he realized the reddish stone steps under his feet were dry. They had been wet where Vardan had presumably trod before him. Turning back down the stair, he found the damp trail led to a landing on the third floor of the main tower. There were two doorways on the landing. To the right, an open square room appeared to be used for storage. Sacks of dry goods and wooden crates were stacked. A winch and pulley system was rigged near a large double-door on the front side of the tower.

On the opposite side of the landing, a smaller door stood open in the round tower, shedding some light into the otherwise dark store room. A sopping wet, rust-colored cloak lay in the lit doorway's threshold.

He picked up the cloak and shook it. It was heavy with rainwater, but had a hole in it that looked like it had been caused by fire. There was nothing in its pockets that Raleigh could find with a quick inspection. He spread it out on a crate in the store room and then went through the smaller door.

Inside, was a small semi-circular room, dimly lit by glowing spheres held in sconces on either side of the doorway.

Behind the door, Vardan, his brown hair and maroon robes soaked through and through, lay on his side, face against the curved wall of streaked red and yellow stone.

Raleigh knelt to check on him. Something that looked like a huge iron nail or spike was clenched in his cold, dead fist. Raleigh rolled him onto his back and saw that his eyes were wide open, now staring blankly at the ceiling. The dead Talanth's pupils were dilated to a point that his vacant eyes looked like onyx.

Vardan's storm-laden maroon robes had a hole over his chest. Like the wet cloak, unlikely as it seemed, it looked to be burned through.

Raleigh looked around the little room. Dominating the west end was something that looked like a large stone basin, but turned on its side. It looked to be made of the same kind of polished white stone as the pillar in the undercroft that served as the hub of the three portal arches. Beneath that, two rectangular brass plates were set in the wooden floor, a couple feet from the wall.

On the opposite side of the small room was an altar of sorts, of the same white stone. Four small rectangular basins with a number of apparent drain holes were carved into its top surface and in a number of nooks in the wall above were large spikes similar to the one in Vardan's hand.

The contrivances in the room certainly looked interesting, but more pressing matters concerned Raleigh just then.

He continued up the stairs and saw light behind a cracked door on one of the upper landings.

"Davis? Reg?" Raleigh called out.

"In here," came the gravely voice of old Davis Talanth.

Raleigh pushed the door the rest of the way open and stepped into some sort of laboratory.

"Don't touch anything," Davis said, moving towards Raleigh. "Vardan works with some pretty toxic substances in here."

"Vardan is dead." Raleigh stated simply.

Davis stopped and stared blankly for a moment. "I beg your pardon."

"I found him dead in a small round room across from a storage room. This, I found outside," Raleigh produced the formerly magical amulet from his pocket.

Davis shook his head. "I don't understand. Dead. How?"

"I don't know, but he went outside before whatever happened to him. It looks like he was... I don't know, burned? Hit by lightning? There's a hole through his cloak and his robe. Looks burned, but he was soaked through from going out in the storm."

"Show me."

Raleigh led Davis down the stairs to the third floor and into the small round room where Vardan's wet corpse lay.

Davis knelt and inspected the body. "He was my nephew. A good lad. Promising future," he muttered. "A good lad. Tremendously intelligent. What a crying waste..."

Raleigh stood silently in the doorway.

"Appears to me, he was struck by lightning. Doesn't make sense, though," Davis went on as he examined Vardan's onyx-black and wide-open eyes. "How could he make it up here to die if he was struck by lighting outside? That amulet, too…"

Raleigh stood silent.

"That amulet held a strong protective magic." Davis shook his head. "I don't understand." He pulled Vardan's robes open, revealing a massive, blackened wound on his chest.

"Could the amulet itself have caused the burns?" Raleigh finally spoke.

"Don't see how," Davis said. "Unless…"

"Unless…" Raleigh prompted.

"I don't know. Could be something about this storm. Something more going on. This tower is more than a simple watchtower. It could even be the reason for this storm, I suppose. Maybe. The tower or the area around it. I don't know." He sat on the floor next to the body.

"How so?"

"Like I was telling you, the fabric between the realms is a bit weaker here. The tower actually holds the fabric together in a way. This tower and the portal beneath it… The portal lets us through, but it's an impassable barrier to the elemental spirits on the other side. Every once in a while, they might get a little feisty, though."

"What's that spike thing in Vardan's hand?"

Davis looked up at Raleigh with a grim expression. "That's to do with all this." he gestured around the room with its large upright basin and strange altar-like pedestal. Don't know why he'd have it. Doesn't make any sense. We only use this room to talk to

23

the Highmage. In a dire emergency. Which is to say, we don't use this room. Not really ever. It's called the Whisper Room. Vardan would have no business in here."

"You can communicate with the Highmage with this?"

"Aye, but it's only to be used in the most dire emergency. The magic is old. So, so old. Much of it is lost. Used to be part of a much bigger system, I think."

"And it's never been used?"

"Well, Vardan has certainly never used it. I have. Twice. Once when I was taught how to contact the Capitol with it, and once when there was a bit of a local uprising, yonder." Davis gestured vaguely. "The Lord Highmage was not pleased to be disturbed about that. Not at all." Davis paused. "None of this makes much sense. Where's his cloak?"

Raleigh turned to fetch it from the store room. Davis accepted it from him and briefly inspected it, poking a finger through the hole in the front. He draped it over his nephew's body.

"Does Reginald know about this, yet?"

"No. I came straight away, looking for you when I found Vardan here. There's something else." Raleigh was hesitant, but went on after a thoughtful pause. "There's something happening with the portal."

"Something?" Davis glanced up to the shadows around the ceiling of the Whisper Room. The runes carved up there were a mirror of the runes down in the great hall. The rune representing the portal was dark at the moment, but a glint of reddish light was chasing around the carving of the perimeter rune.

Raleigh decided not to mention his solo return to the undercroft. "I saw the portal rune flickering with bluish light in the sitting room downstairs – the one you said hasn't illuminated in your lifetime, I believe – just after you went looking for Vardan."

24

"I… um… I see. I'll need to find Reg and we'll need to do something with Vardan. Something proper for him," Davis said. His face was ashen, his jaw clenched. He seemed torn between duty and grief.

"I'll fetch him," Raleigh volunteered.

"Oh. Will you? Good."

Visitors in the Night

Raleigh went up and then down the tower looking for Reg and Lana and finally found them on the ground floor by the hearth.

"We have company," Lana announced as Raleigh entered the room.

"More company, yes," said Reg. "I've allowed their passage."

Raleigh noticed that the perimeter runes by the ceiling he'd seen glinting with bright red light earlier were now serenely glowing with a softer purple hue.

He was about to speak when the main entry slowly scraped open, letting cold, blasting wind and the sound of rain and thunder into the formerly warm and quiet space.

A moment later, two hooded men tentatively entered the foyer, looking around cautiously. One had his hand on the hilt of a short sword at his belt. Both were clad in heavy cloaks that on scrutiny were brown but soaked as they were, appeared black at first glance.

"Welcome, friends. Please come in and find shelter in our tower," Reg called out, stepping towards the new arrivals.

Two women followed the men into the hall. Their own fine clothes were equally soaked and despite the wealth suggested by their quality, they were clearly common folk.

The heavy metal door closed behind them all with a thud.

"You have our thanks," said one of the men as he pulled back his hood revealing a heavy head of long, wet gray hair. "I'm Gavin DeVon." Gavin looked to be close to age with Davis, maybe older. He looked somewhat frail, perhaps in diminished health. He introduced the others, "My brother Brune, and our servants."

"Well met, my lords," said Reg. "I'm Reginald Partha. My companions are the Lady Lana Arcana and Lord Raleigh Talanth. The lord of this tower, Davis Talanth bids you shelter and welcome."

Brune let go of his sword to remove his hood as well and nodded. "Thank you, Lord Partha and well met, my lords and lady," he said.

The DeVon brothers were far removed from one another in age and visage. Raleigh didn't think they looked much like family, but the DeVons were a mysterious clan he'd had little interaction with.

While Gavin appeared considerably older and somewhat delicate, with pale, rheumy eyes, Brune had a strong face and prominent jaw with blazing blue eyes and black hair.

"A pleasure, my lords," Raleigh said. He had urgent business with Reg, but he realized he'd have to suffer patiently through the formalities of meeting and greeting magi of other clans. That little bit of ceremonial pleasantry was important.

The Empire was governed by twelve clans of magi, held together by a tenuous alliance – an alliance that had been broken to universally disastrous consequence in the past. Each clan was led by one elder chieftain, who had a seat on the Council of Magi and from their number was elected an emperor of sorts who was called the Highmage. The council settled disputes and enacted laws as necessary. That government structure of republican democracy and shared power mostly kept peace and order, but there were old grudges that ran deep. Mistrust was commonplace among several of the clans. Clashes still occurred – some more dire than others.

The Schism was by far he greatest and most destructive of all the clan wars, but there had been other deadly conflicts, Raleigh knew. It was an area of history that was of particular interest to him. So, he well understood the importance of protocol.

Once all the gestures had been properly made, both grand and polite, Reg saw the new guests to the kitchen. He provisioned them with warm mead and dry clothes and promises to provide anything else they might require that was within his power.

Finally, Raleigh saw an opportunity to pull him and Lana aside.

"Vardan is dead," he said in hushed tones once he'd coaxed them into the round tower stair. "Davis is with his body upstairs. We aren't exactly sure what happened, but I think there may be a hostile presence about the tower."

"Oh my dear," Reg said, stunned. "My master is dead? How? Do you think...?" Reg nodded towards the kitchen.

"No idea," Raleigh replied quickly. "Perhaps."

Lana was shaken. "I imagined we'd found safety here," she said. "What if they are to do with Vardan's death? It seems they've arrived just as he died. Allowing them in to the tower could be putting us all in danger."

"My lady, you have just arrived here, yourself and nothing was amiss before then... well, except for the storm of course. And it was Lord Raleigh here who says he found Vardan dead. I'm not saying... Just saying."

Lana nodded.

"Remain vigilant." Raleigh said.

"I have to..." Reg began, glancing up the stairs.

"Yes. Hurry. Go." Raleigh prompted.

Reg made haste away and up the spiraling steps to find his deceased master and Lord Davis.

Raleigh gestured for Lana to follow and they made their way down the stairs. On the main floor, Raleigh pointed out the runes around the ceiling and quickly explained what he knew of them. There were no longer any lights flickering in the carvings, though.

"Yes, I understand the runes," Lana replied casually.

Raleigh looked at her sidelong then stopped and explained again in more detail.

Lana rolled her eyes a bit. "Thank you. Very useful," she replied.

"Yes. So, let me know if you see any lights in those carvings," Raleigh said.

"I promise I will."

"Good. Alright, well, let's get to know the new guests, then."

Lana followed Raleigh back up to the kitchen.

The servant women stood silently to either side of the hearth and the mismatched Devon brothers sat at the table, drinking mulled wine. All had fresh blankets draped over their shoulders, courtesy of Reg.

Raleigh could see the aura of magic energy around Brune, the younger of the brothers, but he was puzzled by Gavin. Magi couldn't always clearly perceive the aura of a much more advanced mage especially in the light, but in Raleigh's experience, there was usually at least a glimmer of something. He could see that the dagger on Gavin's belt possessed a magical aura, but From Gavin himself, he sensed nothing, like he was a just another commoner.

There were of course, ways to conceal a magic aura, but Raleigh couldn't imagine any reason to go to the trouble of employing such tricks under these circumstances.

The elder DeVon noticed Raleigh. "Thank you for the wine and shelter," he said, looking up.

"No need to thank me, my lord. I'm as much a guest here as yourselves. My companion Lana and I came here seeking shelter from the storm too."

"I see. But you are a Talanth." Gavin rubbed at the corner of his eye.

"Well, yes. Of course, I'm related to the lord of the tower. He's a great, great uncle or something like that."

"Were you on the river as well, then?"

"No. We were crossing the broken lands."

"Dangerous territory," Brune, the younger DeVon put in.

"Indeed, but the river seems to have proven just as treacherous. What brought you this way in such terrible weather?" Raleigh responded.

Brune was about to speak, but a subtle gesture from Gavin interrupted him and the elder brother spoke for their party.

"We have business in Bloussen. There was no storm when we set out and though the weather became unpleasant, the river was perfectly navigable. It wasn't a concern until we reached the horseshoe bend in the canyon. Then, the trouble began," Gavin explained.

"There's a terrible tempest just to the east of here," Lana said. "It only would have worsened beyond the bend. Three of my friends died out there."

Brune spoke up. "Our vessel is normally more than capable, but something queer happened when we got near this tower. The magic bound to the boat became erratic. That vessel has been in our family for generations and always served us well. Now, I fear its power is lost."

Gavin shot his younger brother a disapproving look.

The DeVons tended to keep to themselves. Raleigh guessed the elder brother considered the less said about their clan's assets, the better. Still, Raleigh's curiosity pressed him to pry a little. "Elemental magic?"

Brune seemed reluctant to elaborate further. "Old magic," was all he'd say and even with that, Gavin scowled.

"I see," said Raleigh, thoughtfully. "So you came ashore beneath the tower?"

"Crashed into this rock is more like it," Gavin said. "It was a chore to get up that muddy slope from the river in the storm."

"Did someone come down to help you up?" Raleigh asked.

"No." Said Gavin.

"Did you meet or see anyone outside the tower when you arrived?"

"No. Why do you ask?"

"It's my cousin. He went outside just before you arrived. Vardan Talanth. About my size, brown hair, beard, a bit older than me…"

"No. I told you. We didn't see anyone."

"It's just that he's turned up dead." Raleigh went on.

Gavin cast his watery eyes downward. "When?"

"Just as you were arriving," Raleigh said. "Under quite mysterious circumstances."

"Now see here, Talanth!" Brune stood up from the table, pointing a finger at Raleigh.

"Calm, brother," Gavin spoke softly, dabbing a stray tear with the cuff of his sleeve. "Lord Talanth isn't accusing us, surely."

"No. Accusations? Of course not, my lords. I mean only to gather information, and to inform you that we may have something other than the storm to worry about. You've arrived at a very unhappy moment, I'm afraid. Reginald didn't even know yet when he admitted you and he was Lord Vardan's apprentice."

"I'm so sorry to hear of this tragedy," Gavin said as he gestured for his younger brother to sit back down. "You have our deepest condolences and we are at your service and to the master of the tower who gave us welcome, as well."

Raleigh was fairly certain Davis hadn't even been aware his welcome had been extended by Reg. "I'm sure that's appreciated. Reginald has just gone to help Lord Davis with the body, I believe," Raleigh said.

"Our servants will assist," Brune volunteered.

Raleigh and Lana exchanged a brief glance.

"Yes, of course," Gavin agreed. "Tanya. Inga. Go and offer your assistance to the lord of the tower." He waved his hand vaguely.

The two commoners looked to each other uncertainly.

"My lords, your gesture is surely most kind, but I think the keepers of the tower have the situation in hand. Let your servants get warm and dry by the fire, first," Raleigh suggested.

"Nonsense," Brune said, a little too loudly. "They are more than capable. Good strong women, aren't you?"

"Yes my lord," Tanya and Inga said in unison.

"Go on." Brune swept his hand towards the door. The two shuffled tentatively to the doorway.

Lana made a gesture upwards to give them some clue of a direction and the servants disappeared into the darkness of the round tower stair.

Bumps in the Shadows

"How are we supposed to be any help to two magi moving a body?" Inga whispered to her companion as they made their way up the spiraling stone stairway.

"Always questions, with you," Tanya said. "Speak less. Observe more. Just do as I do."

"I mean, can't they just spirit the dead away, or bring them back to life, for that matter?"

"Don't say such things, girl. You don't know what you're saying," Tanya admonished.

As a young girl, Inga used to dream of the wonders and splendor that must have been within the Devonshire keep, but she never actually thought that she'd see for herself. In the two years since she'd been accepted as a household servant to the lords of Devonshire, she'd seen more wonders than her naive girlhood imagination could conjure, but there were frightful things as well.

There were times Inga regretted that her impossible wish to see how the lords and ladies of the land lived had actually come true. Sloshing out of the boat in the storm and climbing the steep and muddy slope up to the tower was far from the worst of it.

Tanya stopped at a landing and peered into a dark store room. On the opposite side of the landing was a smaller circular room, but when Tanya looked in, she said, "oh, no." and turned away immediately.

Inga saw that there were odd-looking contraptions within. Magic things, probably, that they had no business with.

Seeing no one about, Tanya led on up to the next level of the tower and there found a dark and empty bedroom, then more beds on the floor above that.

Up the dark stair they went until they heard voices from a room on the sixth level of the tower. They stopped on the landing outside the open door.

"Who's there?" came a gruff voice.

"Tanya and Inga, my lord. Our masters sent us to lend assistance if it please you," Tanya answered.

"Come in here, girls, but touch nothing. You understand? There are toxic substances in this laboratory. Nothing for touching by common folk!"

"Yes, my lord," Tanya said as she stepped one foot through the doorway, her hands clasped demurely before her.

"I'm Lord Davis Talanth and this is… This was the deceased's ward and apprentice, Lord Reginald Partha."

The two servants curtsied.

"Can't imagine why your master would send two girls to help with a corpse," Davis grumbled.

Tanya and Inga stood silently.

"Very well. I had in mind bringing poor Vardan up here to the laboratory, but I've just had another idea." Davis said, then turned to Reginald. "With this storm, it looks like it'll be a while before we could bury Vardan. What about using the cold storage? Then we don't have to take him all the way up here for embalming, either."

Reginald nodded. "I'd rather we cleared all the food out of there before we put Lord Vardan in, though," he said.

"Good. Go show these girls the store room and they can move all the food to the kitchen. We'll use it all anyway, with these extra mouths, for certain," Davis instructed.

Lord Partha nodded and led the two servants into the main stairway. Some thumping and banging resounded from below and grew louder as they descended. They stopped at a landing on the third level where both the store room and the room with the odd contraptions were. He nodded towards the smaller room. "Vardan is in there," he said sadly, then led them into the square store room. It was dark and still, sparsely populated with crates and sacks and shadows.

Lord Partha picked up a glass sphere from a ledge by the door and tossed it into the air. It stopped about in the middle of the room, near the high ceiling, just hanging in the air as if suspended by a string. It illuminated, chasing the shadows back to cobwebbed corners.

On one side of the room, there was a block and tackle system before two huge doors that were banging and rattling against a savage wind that seemed dead set on prying its way in. On the wall opposite was a large chest. The red-robed young mage beckoned for the servants to follow him as he approached that.

Louder, rapid knocks sounded from the big doors, startling Inga but Lord Partha glanced that way briefly, and seemed unconcerned. The servants followed him and he opened the chest. Inside were varied cuts of meat, some salted, some wrapped in cloth.

"Magic in this box keeps it cold and that slows decay and preserves the meat longer," Reginald explained. "It should work the same for my poor master, Lord Vardan, until we can bury him. I guess that's what we all are in the end... Meat." He was silent for a while and seemed lost in thought. "Take all of these meats down to the kitchen," he said when his senses came back to the here and now. "There is a cupboard by the hearth that should serve to store it all until we eat it."

"Yes, my lord," Tanya said.

Inga only nodded, following the senior servant's lead.

As they were bending to begin the chore, the huge double wooden doors suddenly slammed open exposing the store room to the raging storm outside. Lightning flashed brilliantly as the wind blasted freezing, hard rain into the store room.

It became cold as the dead of winter in an instant. Inga could see her own breath. Then she noticed a blanket of frost spreading rapidly across the floor from the open chest and she gasped.

The wind grew stronger and whipped about the room.

Reginald's voluminous red robes snapped against the gusting wind as he moved to re-secure the big wooden doors and suddenly he was gone – as if flung by an unseen but mighty hand, straight out the storage room doors and into the stormy night.

The astonished servants could only gape at the impossible as the young Partha just up and flew away to into obscurity.

The space became somewhat calmer once Lord Partha had flown out the doors. The lightning still flashed and thunder clapped. The wind lessened, though it still bore rain into the room.

The frost ceased its rapid spread from the chest and had already begun to melt away.

"We should close the doors," Inga said, when the initial shock of it all began to subside. She turned towards the opening.

"Are you crazy?" Tanya yelled. "Didn't you see what I just saw? Didn't you see what just happened to Lord Partha?!"

Inga tentatively inched towards the opening in the wall, intending to look for Lord Partha on the ground, three stories below, but Tanya grabbed her roughly from behind.

"No, Inga! Stay back! Come with me. This business is for the magi."

Tanya was right, of course. Inga saw the sense of her words.

She followed Tanya hastily down the stairs to the kitchen. There, they found their masters still conversing with Lord Raleigh Talanth and Lady Lana Arcana and dared to interrupt them.

"Lord Partha is dead," Inga blurted.

She felt like she'd just stepped onto a stage without ever rehearsing her lines as all the magi in the room turned their attention to the novice servant.

"He flew. He flew out... out... into the storm," Inga stammered.

Tanya came to her rescue. "My lords, The big doors in the storage room blew open and when Lord Partha went to secure them, a mighty wind swept him out. We dared not look out for him, lest we get swept away too."

Raleigh Talanth leapt to his feet.

"We must go out and find him," Lady Arcana said, also standing.

"If there is a dangerous foe lurking about the tower, as you suggest, Lord Talanth, we should exercise caution," Lord Gavin put in. "Perhaps it would be unwise to go brashly bursting out the main door of the tower into the unknown."

"Indeed. Was Reginald murdered, perhaps?" Lord Brune posited.

Young Raleigh Talanth seemed to dismiss the debating of the DeVon brothers without consideration as he dashed out of the kitchen and down the winding stairs. Lady Arcana followed, with only a quick glance at the Lords DeVon.

The elder brother gave a small shrug. "I suppose we'd seem callused and unappreciative guests if we failed to offer our support," he said.

Lord Brune turned his palms up. "Tanya, go find Lord Davis and tell him what has transpired. Inga, come with us." He led the way, with less haste, down the stairs.

Down on the ground floor, the hearth blazed bright and hot, contrasted by a cold, damp wind blowing from the entry corridor.

Lord Raleigh and Lady Lana had already gone out and the big metal door was still open.

Inga trailed several paces behind her masters as they proceeded down the hall. The wind and cold intensified with each step and they stopped at the pegs in the wall to don their meager cloaks before crossing the tower's threshold.

Outside, the stormy atmosphere was unrelenting, with lightning loud and rapid.

Inga stood hesitantly just beyond the tower door and was grateful to see that the young Talanth and his black-robed Arcana companion were already making their staggering way back to the tower with a lame figure she assumed was Lord Partha supported between them.

Everyone gathered back in the great hall before the blazing fire, shedding dripping cloaks and wringing water from their hair.

The great tower door closed of its own accord as Inga's masters helped lay Lord Partha upon the divan. He was alive but ashen and he appeared in considerable pain.

Tanya and the elder Talanth, Lord Davis came into the room.

"Here, now, let me see the boy," said Lord Davis as he pushed through the group to kneel by the divan. "What happened, now? Are you injured?"

Lord Partha looked strained to even breathe, but managed to reply, "I think my legs are broken. I can't walk on them. My chest..." he coughed weakly, wincing in obvious pain from the exertion.

"Alright, lad. Alright. You'll be alright," said Lord Davis. "We'll get you patched up." He patted Reginald's shoulder, gently.

"Let's make sure all the ways in and out of the tower are secure," said Lord Raleigh Talanth. "This might not have been an accident."

The Fog of Time

Reg had been carefully brought up to his own bed, stripped and examined. One leg was broken at the shin. Davis determined that his other leg was sound, except torn ligaments around the knee. At least two of his ribs were cracked, accounting for his painful and labored breathing.

Lana helped Davis set splints for his legs and bind the young Partha's superficial wounds.

"I'm something of an alchemist," Brune DeVon had said, digging though a pouch at his hip. He offered a vial containing a potent potion to ease Reginald's pain and help him sleep.

Once Reg was settled and drifting into a drug-induced slumber, the DeVons adjourned to the kitchen, where they set their serving girls to work preparing a meal for everyone. There was a surplus of meat to be used.

Raleigh, meanwhile had wrestled the storage room doors closed and latched, then twice made rounds of every inch of the tower that he could access looking for any loose latches or bars that could compromise their security.

He was impressed with the design of the tower and realized much of it was warded against intrusion by magic.

The storage room doors were an apparent exception, so Raleigh revisited that room. The big wooden doors, along with the block and tackle pulley system installed above them were probably later additions, he reasoned. Perhaps some former masters of the tower had decided to bring in peasant servants who could benefit from such a device. Magi prestigious enough to govern a tower like this would surely possess a simple levitation spell to move heavy goods up into the store room.

As he considered it, Raleigh was pretty sure storage wasn't even the room's intended purpose. Whatever it was originally used for had probably been long forgotten, though.

After a closer examination of the seemingly less-secure doors, he called to mind a spell that would help brace them for the time being. Within the tower, there was an abundance of mana for him to draw upon.

"Sigelu ci tiujn pordojn kune," he intoned as he traced the shapes of magic symbols onto the doors with a finger.

Next, he turned his attention to the cold storage chest, which had been emptied and now seemed quite disenchanted. He'd been told that magic kept its contents cool, but there was no trace of an aura about the box that Raleigh could discern and it felt no cooler than the ambient air of the dimly-lit room, although that was a bit chilly.

Raleigh moved on and after he had finished a third round of the tower, he found Davis working on some sort of poultices up in the laboratory.

"Where's Lana?" Raleigh asked.

"I believe the young lady went for a lie down. Can't say I blame her. This has been tiring business, m'lad."

"No question." Raleigh was plain. Then, shifting topics, he said, "This is truly a remarkable tower."

"Aye. No question," Davis smirked as he ground some herbs under his pestle.

"There are some who would say the architect was Ranius himself," Raleigh put forth.

Davis continued his work. "Some might say, aye."

"I suppose he's credited with a multitude of feats, though. Ranius Talanth, greatest artificer of all time... So revered as to seem almost mythic..."

"Oh, he was real enough, no mistake. He existed and that's certain," Davis looked up from his labors. "Make no mistake."

The serious turn of Davis' tone wasn't lost on Raleigh. "Of course."

"Still, you have a fair point." Davis added. "Surely not every little trinket with the name of Ranius attached was actually his work."

Raleigh sank into a comfy, over-stuffed leather chair, nodded his agreement, yawned and watched Davis work in silence. "Is there anything I can do to help you?" He said after a while, rubbing at one eye and then the other.

"No. Thank you. I've got this well in hand. Old recipes for healing. Should help the boy some."

Raleigh nodded sleepily. "I have a theory," he said.

"Yes?"

"The DeVon's purported magic boat... the cold storage chest... Elemental magic, no doubt."

"Uh huh." Davis was mixing a sticky paste.

"In the undercroft, a portal to the three realms..."

"Yes..." Davis continued stirring his pungent mixture.

"This ungodly storm... It's all related, don't you think? Elemental spirits. You said they get 'feisty' sometimes."

"Feisty? Is that what you call all this?" Davis waved his mortar around as lightning flashed through the otherwise dark, rain-streaked windows of the laboratory.

"Your word, Lord Davis."

"What do you reckon they're after, then? The elementals?"

"Us, it would seem. Or something we're in the way of." Raleigh rubbed his eyes, feeling more fatigued by the moment as he tried to cling to an increasingly slippery train of thought. "Something in the tower?"

"Might be."

"The tower itself, perhaps?"

"Maybe, aye. No doubt there's value in this old tower. Some of the ancient pacts between magi and the spirits were probably made here," Davis said. "I daresay, some of our spells would not exist if not for some of the goings on around here. Great and mighty pacts were probably wrought here, long ago."

"Would that be cause to attack the tower?"

Davis thought a minute. "I can't think how it would be. What do you make of our other guests, then? The DeVons?"

"Victims of circumstance," Raleigh posited. "Wrong place at the wrong time, like Lana and myself. Their boat, enchanted with elemental magic carried them dutifully along the river until they neared the tempest and it suddenly rebelled, perhaps joining in with the very spirits that menace us now. Not unlike your cold storage chest." Raleigh's was fighting to keep his eyes open, but he continued his thought. "Somehow the elementals bound to these contrivances broke their enchantments. Maybe the very spirit that used to keep your meat cold was what flung poor Reg out the high doors."

Davis looked thoughtful. "Could be something to your theory." He glanced at Raleigh. "Here. I'm going to apply these poultices to poor Reg. Why don't you get some rest yourself for now? This tower has stood, protecting these lands and its occupants for centuries. We'll all be safe enough for now – as long as we're all bolted inside and mindful. You did well to check the perimeter and I have a mind to make my own rounds as well. Nothing at all will bother you in here."

Raleigh nodded wearily as he stood. "Rest is a good idea," he said, shuffling towards the stair. "I put a seal on the storage room doors. It's strong enough to stymie most mortals. Elementals? I don't know."

"Good lad. We'll be safe enough for now, trust. Look, there are some things about this tower I suppose I should be telling you," Davis added, stopping Raleigh in his tracks. "After dinner, I reckon. Get your rest for now."

Raleigh nodded again and proceeded down the dark, winding stairs.

What Lies Beneath

The hearth in the cluttered square kitchen burned hot and bright.

Grateful for dry clothes and a warm secure room, Inga began work on preparing dinner for everyone as her master had instructed. Of course, she was obliged to obey instructions from either of the DeVon brothers, but it was Brune she answered most frequently and directly to. Tanya was the older brother's servant and had been for some years. Inga had only more recently been brought into the DeVon household.

It was on account of her father that the mage lords of Devonshire had taken her in. He was exceptionally talented at working with leather and as such, had secured a coveted job in the Devonshire book bindery. That was the DeVon family business. They ran vast vineyards too, with thousands of peasants working the lands for them.

Working in the bindery put Inga's father inside the walls, as it were, and closer to the DeVons, themselves. He'd carefully parlayed his position into gaining favor for his daughter as well.

It had seemed like favor at the time.

Sometimes Inga missed her simpler peasant's life. She'd gained privilege, no doubt, but the mage lords were frightening at times and dealt with frightful business.

She didn't always understand what her masters were talking about, but she grasped enough to realize it was usually best to pretend that she'd heard little and understood less. Except when spoken to directly, of course.

There was no shortage of intrigue and scandal within the walls of Devonshire. Her lords, Gavin and Brune carried it everywhere, like baggage. There was always a sort of tension between them.

Those two lords now sat at the table sipping wine and paying Inga no mind while she worked.

"Why so glum, brother?" Inga's black-haired master said. "I feel invigorated. Can't you feel that?"

That seemed true. Even Lord Brune's blue eyes seemed brighter — as if they had a light their own.

"Feel what? Gavin shrugged. "Frustration? We're so close. And now, this."

"You're close, you mean."

"Our plan will benefit you as well. You'll find the new arrangement quite to your benefit, I'm sure! If we can get to Bloussen, that is."

"Your plan," Brune corrected, "But can't you sense that? There's a convergence of force lines, here. At least two. Maybe three or more. With power like this…"

"Yes, yes. Of course, I can sense it, you fool," Gavin snapped. "But, there's more than one kind of power, you know. We have to get to that clan meeting."

"There will be other chances if we can't make this one," Brune said with a casual shrug.

"It must be now," Gavin replied sharply. Then he took a deep breath and closed heavy eyes with dark circles around them. A tear escaped and ran down his cheek. Smoothing his long gray hair, he said, "Listen. As time passes, our chances of success diminish. I can't explain everything just now, but trust me on this. The time to strike is now."

"As you say," Brune took a sip of his wine.

"It's probably why they located this tower where they did," Gavin shifted topics. "At least in part…"

"What?"

"The power you sense… That we sense… The power here. The force lines that converge here."

"Oh. Of course," Brune waved his cup vaguely around the kitchen. "With all the mana at our disposal, perhaps there is some spell that could aid our travel?"

"Do you think I haven't thought of that? I'm thinking about that," Gavin snapped.

Inga looked up from the vegetables she was cutting when Tanya entered the kitchen. Her masters, Lords Brune and Gavin DeVon broke off their conversation to also regard the other servant.

"My lords," Tanya began. "The Talanths were coming out of the laboratory, so I had to make haste back down here to avoid being seen and I don't have much to report."

"Rather than telling us how little you have, why not just provide what you do?" Lord Brune suggested cooly.

"Yes, My lord." Tanya came further into the room, closing the door behind her.

"No. Leave that," Lord Gavin said. "Looks suspicious."

Tanya turned and opened the door again, but crossed midway into the room before resuming her report. "The Talanths do not seem to believe we are in any way responsible for Lord Vardan's death or Lord Partha's injuries. I heard nothing to suggest any suspicion is being cast this way," she began.

"Good," said Lord Brune.

"Actually, Lord Raleigh Talanth said he believed our party to be victims of circumstance like himself."

"Go on," said Brune.

"I wasn't able to listen long, my lord, but Lord Davis was working on a salve or something for Lord Partha, I believe and they spoke of elemental spirits."

"Elementals?" Lord Gavin put in.

"Yes, m'lord. I gathered that they believe that has something to do with Lord Partha's accident and they even said maybe it's why the boat ran aground."

"Indeed? What else did they postulate about elemental spirits?" the elder DeVon asked.

"Postulate, my lord?"

"Make assumptions," Gavin explained.

"Oh. Yes. They said something about a portal in the undercroft that was somehow connected to the boat and the storm and the cold chest as well. They said it might all be connected and something about this tower, itself, but I didn't hear that clearly or understand it. They were coming and I didn't want to be found listening…"

"Of course," Lord Brune waved a dismissive hand.

"Interesting," Lord Gavin said.

Lord Brune nodded. "So, there's a portal to an elemental realm beneath the tower, it sounds like."

"Indeed, it sounds likely," replied Gavin. "There's more to this tower than meets the eye. It's not just a bulwark against those wildlands. Perhaps it guards much more than that and perhaps there could be something to use to advance our plans."

"Your plan. I think it's time we investigated more of this tower for ourselves, though." Brune suggested. "surreptitiously, of course."

Inga didn't know what "surreptitiously" meant and she guessed Tanya didn't either, but neither asked.

Lord Gavin stood. "You girls finish up on dinner for everyone. We're going to take a walkabout. If anyone asks after us, tell them we've gone down to the hall to recline by the fire."

Brune got up from his seat as well and followed his older brother out into the main stairway.

Tanya moved closer to Inga to help her with the cooking. They had moved all the meat from the no-longer-cold box to a cupboard in the kitchen, so Tanya found a suitable portion to cut up for stew, as she surmised Inga was making.

"What are they going to do with the body?" Inga asked.

"I don't know. Embalm him, probably," Tanya answered as she picked out a big knife.

"What's that?"

"It's a way to stop a body from rotting, for a while. So it doesn't stink up the place," Tanya said quietly. "I guess there's no crypts or catacombs under this tower, so they have to wait to bury him."

"What is in the undercroft, though? What's a portal?" Inga asked her more experienced colleague.

"It's a sort of doorway," Tanya answered as she trimmed a big hunk of red meat. "Might be magical."

"What's an elemental realm?"

"The elemental spirits," Tanya began hesitantly, somewhat uncertain. "They're like demons that the magi make bargains with or sometimes even enslave, I think. They command the winds, and fire, too. The realms are like a shadow of our world. It's where the elementals come from."

Inga shivered. "So we're stuck in this tower with demons attacking it and there's a doorway to Hell right underneath us?"

Tanya gave her frightened companion a grim look and nodded slowly before resuming her work on the stew. Tanya apparently hadn't yet considered it like that herself.

The Shadow on the High Walk

Lana woke after a too-short slumber, but her mind was racing and she knew it wouldn't be possible to get back to sleep. Her dreams had been disturbing, anyway.

Checking that they were mostly dry, she pulled her black robes on over the borrowed clothes she'd worn to bed and shuffled across the darkened room to the door.

Heavy curtains blocked the flickering storm light and the main stair was quiet, save for a dull hum resonating from the bell faintly vibrating at the top of the tower. The hum grew more distinct when she opened the door into the round tower, but the thick stone walls dampened the continuous thunder booming outside.

Lana made her way down the curving steps to the kitchen and there found the two servants of the DeVon brothers. They were preparing a meal of some kind with their backs to the door. No one else was about.

"Where is everyone?" Lana asked from the doorway. Both the women jumped at the unexpected sound. After a moment, they turned stiffly to regard her.

"I couldn't say for certain, my lady," said Tanya, the brown-haired commoner who was the older of the two.

"Can't or won't?"

"Our masters may have gone to the great hall downstairs to sit by the fire. I don't know where any of the other magi have gotten off to, my lady."

"Would you like a cup of tea?" the younger one stepped toward the hearth and reached for a kettle that hung over the fire.

"Yes. Thank you," Lana said, stepping fully into the room.

The servant poured her a cup and Lana sat at the table for just a moment, but she felt awkward alone in the kitchen with the two commoners working and decided to take her cup of tea down to the hall. Finding the ground floor vacant, Lana sat on the divan alone, before the blaze in the great hearth. She rubbed the sleep from her eyes and sipped her hot tea.

As her mind grew more awake, Lana contemplated the situation.

There had been some grim circumstances, but surely, the tower had been built to protect its occupants. *As long as we remain vigilant, we will all come out of this storm — those of us who remain, that is.*

A red light flickered near the ceiling.

Lana looked up with a grimace. It was the perimeter rune. Someone, or something was lurking on the tower grounds.

Could just be the DeVon brothers out exploring, Lana considered. *In the storm, though?*

Could just be vengeful spirits trying to break in to the tower and kill us all.

Lana put her cup down on the floor and made for the stairs. Round and round and up and up she went, until, feeling somewhat winded, she reached the landing for the lookout room, eight stories up.

Taking deep breaths, she stepped into the room that was almost surrounded by windows. Lightning flashed dazzlingly. The bell from the nearby belfry hummed its tone.

Lana paced slowly around the big, empty chamber, peering out through the thick, masterfully crafted glass. Despite bright bolts of lightning frequently framing the silhouettes of nearby features, like the shape of merlons around the parapet walk, the storm obfuscated much of the tower's environs. The ground, the river and canyon mostly melded into one inky black void below. Rain streaked down the window panes and mists danced around the tower's heights.

Something didn't look right.

What was that?

Lana moved closer to one window, where an out-of-place glimpse of movement caught her eye for a moment. From the back of her brain, her mind hinted she'd seen the shape of a hooded man out on the parapet, but there was no one there. Just rain, fog and flashing light.

"There," she said aloud, turning towards another window. *There it was again. A something. A someone?*

She hurried to look out and then, jumped back on the next stroke of lightning. The silhouette of a man stood out there in the raging storm, perfectly still and seeming to stare right back through the window at Lana.

A brilliant flash of lightning dazzled her eyes for a moment and then, the figure was gone.

"Who's out there?" She hollered, but immediately felt foolish. *No one could hear me from out there!*

Pressing up to the thick glass, she tried in vain to again spot the lone figure who stood on the high walk in the punishing rain. From the brief glimpse, the figure had seemed about Vardan's height and build, but that couldn't be. Vardan was dead.

Seeing nothing at the moment, she stepped back to the middle of the room for perspective and glanced all around at the twelve great windows.

Nothing.

She looked at a door that led out onto the parapet walk and briefly considered going out into the gales for a closer look, but thought better of it.

Raleigh and Vardan were about the same height and build. It could just be Raleigh out there, but it could be anything at all and I don't want to get flung from the tower like poor Reg.

Lana decided it would be better to report to the others, what she'd seen. If it was anything at all. It may have been a trick of the light and her agitated imagination. The more she concentrated on what the figure had looked like, the more an impression crept in that it was transparent. Like the mere shape of a man, composed of nothing more substantial than the wind and rain.

Lana discarded that notion. Maybe one of the others would know who was out on the parapet and if not, they could confront the mysterious figure together. She started back down the winding stairs, her hand absently rubbing along the dark reddish stone wall as she went. It was cool and smooth.

One floor below the observation room, there was a library. Luminescence spheres in sconces aside the doorway dimly lit the densely packed bookshelves and lightning flickered through the deep-set windows, but the room was unoccupied.

Down another floor, Lana peered into the dark laboratory on her way past, but saw no one there. In the round tower at that level, there was a sturdy, banded door which she found locked.

Lord Davis seemed pretty free with access to most of the tower so Lana wondered what made that room an exception. *What's kept in there? Something powerful? Valuables? Something shameful?*

Continuing down, she came to the sleeping rooms. There were two floors with bed chambers. The upper one was where Vardan and Reg slept. In the room below were guest beds. Davis slept in a room on the main floor to the side of the entry hall, Lana had learned.

She found the door to Reg's room open and peeked in. There was Davis, knelt beside the ailing young Partha's bed.

"How's he doing?" Lana inquired softly from the doorway.

"He'll be alright," Davis replied.

"Yes. I'll live," Reg spoke for himself.

"Oh. You're awake," Lana said. "I'm glad. You gave us all quite a fright."

"Not so much as I experienced, I shouldn't think!" Reg lifted his head for a moment to look at Lana with a slight wince.

"What happened?"

Reg lowered his head back to the pillow. "It all happened too fast to say for sure," he said. "The big storage doors were banging against the wind and they just blew open all of a sudden. I went to close them, but that's when something got me from behind. I never saw what it was, but it was something fast and strong and cold as ice. It bowled into me, picked me right up off my feet and carried me right outside. I *flew*. Then I was falling. Didn't land very gracefully…"

"An elemental, from the cold box, maybe," Davis grumbled. "It don't keep cold any more, it seems."

Lana felt a chill from that statement. "Do elemental spirits sometimes take the shape of men?"

"Aye." Davis stood. "Saw one, did you?"

"Maybe. I'm not sure."

"That sounds about right. Smells like something's getting ready to be eaten."

Lana sniffed the air. Some savory odor was wafting up through the tower. "I thought I saw a man out on the parapet, but he just vanished before I could get a good look. I had a strange impression that he was made of rain and mist, rather than just surrounded by it."

Davis nodded. "Tell us about it over supper. Here, Reg, I'll bring some up for you. Feeling well enough?"

"I'm fine for now," Reg said. No hurry on the food, but it does smell good. I feel sleepy, still." His eyelids did still look heavy.

"It was a potent potion Lord DeVon gave you," Davis said. "Rest now, then. I'll be back to check on you after a while."

Reg nodded, closed his eyes and turned to press his cheek into the pillow.

Lana followed Davis down the curving stone stairway. "I've been around the tower and secured some areas," the older Talanth said as they descended. "It's tiring work, but I have a couple more tasks in mind. After I sit and eat something."

Lana didn't know what the lord of the tower had in mind exactly, but just nodded silently.

They came into the kitchen, which was already crowded with the tower's full complement. Less poor Reginald, of course. Raleigh sat at the table with the DeVon brothers. The servant girls were dishing up a thick and steaming stew. It smelled delicious enough that Lana almost forgot their rather dire circumstances.

Davis filled a cup with mead from a hot kettle and accepted a plate of stew from Tanya before sitting at the head of the small table. Inga handed a serving to Lana as she sat down next to Raleigh.

"Sounds like they're testing our perimeter," Davis addressed the room after washing a spoonful of stew down with a hearty swig of mulled mead. "Lana saw what I'd reckon was a wind elemental up on the parapet. Good thing she didn't open the door for a closer look, I think." He set his goblet down, put his palms flat on the table and looked to each in turn, before he said sternly, "open no egress to the outside and we have naught to fear."

"But why would elemental spirits want to get in to this tower?" Brune asked.

"To kill us, based on what we've seen so far," Lana said.

"There must be more to it than that. It must be tied to the extraordinary tempest raging outside, and probably the energies that converge here," Gavin said. "So, what's special about this tower? Does it guard more than the realms of mortal men, perhaps?"

He was fishing, but knew more than he let on, Lana was certain. Something about the elder brother's tone didn't sit right with her.

"It guards secrets," Davis replied with a wink.

"I've been thinking about where I found Vardan's body," Raleigh interjected. "Why was he in the Whisper Room?"

"That's a good question," Davis pointed his spoon at Raleigh. "Can't think of any reason he should have been in there."

The DeVon brothers both cocked their heads in unison and Lana had to suppress a snicker. They looked like hounds who heard a word that sounded close to "treats."

Davis sighed. "Ordinarily, I wouldn't be so loose with the details, but I reckon we're all in this bind together and I'll tell you this much. The whisper room is a very old contrivance that allows for ethereal communication with Bloussen. It's only used to talk to the Highmage and although Vardan had a basic understanding of how to contact the Highmage with it, he'd never done it himself and had no reason I can figure to be in the room, but it's where he was found dead."

"You can contact the capitol with this whisper room?" Gavin's raised interest was obvious.

"Yes. Well, it can facilitate communication with the Highmage when he's in his tower."

"Couldn't we use this contrivance to call for assistance?" Gavin suggested.

Davis scoffed. "I wouldn't be so inclined."

"I have other urgent reasons to contact the capitol," Gavin pressed, "but surely you can see that what's happening around this tower could be of interest, as a potential threat to the Empire."

"Hah." Davis scoffed again. "It's true my nephew lost his life due to carelessness and the young Partha was injured — *also* because of carelessness, but I'd hardly call that a threat to the Empire. It's not even a threat to us. I've been seeing to that. We're perfectly safe. This tower was built specifically to resist such things. As long as it's tended properly, nothing can touch us in here."

"You know… Vardan had one of those spike things clenched tight in his fist when I found him," Raleigh put in. "was he trying to invoke the power of the Whisper Room?"

Davis shook his head. "I still don't understand what he thought he was doing in there," he said sadly. "That particular rod isn't even involved in contacting the capitol. I honestly don't know its purpose. Probably for communicating with some other long lost outpost. No reason for Vardan to be messing about with it. None at all."

"Does the Whisper Room serve any other purpose?" Raleigh asked.

Davis looked a bit uncomfortable and he shifted in his seat before taking a swig of mead. "All we need to do is sit tight," he said. "I've seen these elementals get feisty before. They'll rattle some doors and windows and kick up some thunder and then the wind that was puffing up their sails will be exhausted and it'll be all quiet again. They can't maintain a hold on our realm. Not here."

"You've seen it like this before?" Brune was surprised.

"Aye. Well, not to this extent. Some spirit might have a little more steam boiling than usual, but it'll blow over, just like the other times. Of that, I'm certain. There were one or two little details I still meant to see to and then I assure you, the tower will be impregnable. Then, we'll all just sit tight a while, the storm will pass and everyone can get on back to their own business." Davis fixed everyone with a stern gaze that said he was done debating and he rose from his seat. "I'll be off to see to those details, now, so never fear." He stepped towards the door, then turned back. "Raleigh, meet me in my study later if you please."

Raleigh nodded and the elder Talanth disappeared into the dark stairway.

"What do you know about this whisper room, Talanth?" Gavin asked Raleigh rather pointedly. "Do you know how it functions?"

"I do not," Raleigh replied.

"We're on important clan business and time is of the essence," Gavin pressed. "A conduit to the capitol would certainly be of value."

"I don't know anything more about it than you. Only Lord Davis does, evidently. And he doesn't seem at all inclined to invoke its power," said Raleigh. "At least not at the present."

Gavin wiped a stray tear from his cheek. "I surmise we're meant to cower in our beds from whatever menace is lurking in this storm, until it passes and take no action in our defense or to further our own business." Frustration was apparent in the elder DeVon's voice.

"Could be worse," Lana said. "You could be outside the tower."

Gavin glared at her. His younger brother smirked.

"Well, it's good fortune for all of us that Lord Davis extended his hospitality," Raleigh interjected. "The apparent epicenter of the tempest is positively deadly and its full fury is likely to fall soon upon us."

"How much longer can this storm persist?" Gavin wondered aloud.

"Days?" Brune shrugged. "Weeks? It's not a natural storm, by their accounts." he waved vaguely at Raleigh and the doorway their host had disappeared through.

"Well, as much as I'm enjoying your company, I certainly hope it won't be weeks," Raleigh said, rising from his seat. "I've had enough… to eat. Please excuse me." He stepped through the door, disappearing into the round tower stair.

That rusty bastard just left me to the wolves, Lana thought, looking toward the dark stairway. She took a big swig of wine from her cup before raising it. "Who knows any good songs?"

Brotherhood

The magi weren't in much mood for singing and Lana soon also excused herself from the kitchen, claiming fatigue.

After she'd left, and the DeVon Brothers were alone with their servants, the intrigue began in earnest. Inga turned her attention to cleaning up after dinner and, as usual, pretended not to hear or understand any of what her masters were discussing. Tanya was even more practiced at it and was already gathering dishes and utensils into a wash tub.

"I've heard of travel between distant places through the three realms," Gavin said. "If we could access the portal that's said to lie beneath this tower, perhaps we could bypass the storms and reenter our own world a safe distance away – closer to Bloussen, even."

Brune considered this brother's idea for a moment, his stern brow furrowed. "Maybe we could traverse some distance through another plane, but we'd still need a portal to return to our world and I have no such spells at my disposal. Do you?"

Gavin shifted uncomfortably but didn't respond.

"Besides," Brune put in, "entering an elemental realm blind and unprepared could prove even more dangerous than the tempest outside." He gestured towards a window that was just then alive with bright flashes from the relentless storm.

"With some study, we might be able to figure out this whisper room contrivance ourselves," Gavin suggested.

Brune shrugged. "Maybe."

"I don't understand Talanth's reluctance to employ it."

"I do. The Highmage is a busy man. He's not a messenger service, you know. He rules the council and the entire Empire. A storm at the edge of some wildlands is hardly worth his attention. I understand Davis' position, even if it doesn't suit your purposes. Besides being incredibly busy, he's incredibly powerful in more ways than one. One would be a fool to risk getting on his cross side."

"You think it can only contact the Highmage? What about those other outposts Raleigh and Davis were talking about?"

"Sounded defunct, from what little I heard."

"Perhaps if I could study it for a while..." Gavin trailed off before changing topics. "How long can this storm last?"

"You repeat yourself, brother." Brune shrugged. "But there are maelstroms in the western seas that are said to go on forever."

Brune was waxing academic and that comment brought a glaring scowl from his older brother.

"Yes. I forget sometimes that you were a Fiend," Gavin said.

Brune's eyes narrowed. "I'm as much a DeVon as you, *brother*. Though you certainly never let *me* forget my parentage."

Inga unconsciously winced. She'd unfortunately been witness to some frightful arguments – some that had even escalated to a point of terrifying magics being loosed – when the subject of lineage was raised between these brothers.

Gavin, Inga had learned, was born a Trueblood and decades prior had been adopted by Lord Alaric DeVon, who was chieftain of the clan DeVon.

Lord Brune had been born into the clan Fiend, but after exile from his own family, he also found a new adoptive father in Lord

Alaric. Inga shouldn't have known these things and would pretend convincingly that she didn't. She *wished* she didn't. Some knowledge was dangerous to even hold.

Brune had been cast out from clan Fiend. Inga had heard whispered (and only half in jest) that the Fiends were so conniving and ruthless that the demonic creatures called fiends had actually been named after the white-robed clan of magi, rather than the reverse.

If the Fiends had found Brune too terrible for their number, she shuddered to even guess at what her master was capable of.

She had no idea what circumstances had brought Gavin into the DeVon fold, only that he had shed the orange robes of his birth clan long before Brune was adopted and became his younger brother.

"I am the heir apparent and a part of this clan for decades before Father took you in," Gavin snapped. "I'll be your chief elder before long, mind you!"

"That depends, brother."

"Are you having second thoughts? Don't you even think of turning against me."

"Bah!" Brune crossed his arms and turned his face away. "Don't be so dramatic."

"With what I now know about Father, It's impossible that the clan elders will continue to tolerate his leadership. I'll be made chieftain, but we have to get to that meeting or the shutters on our window of opportunity will slam shut!"

"Only for now. If we're delayed, there will be other opportunities." Brune looked back to Gavin. Tears were streaming down the elder brother's face.

"You didn't see it for yourself, Brune. The depths of evil I witnessed was almost unfathomable, but so is Father's power. Time isn't on our side."

Inga couldn't tell if the tears on Gavin's face were from sadness, rage or just overflow from his typically watery eyes. She regretted that she'd even glanced in his direction and quickly resumed her work cleaning up with Tanya.

For her part, Tanya had quickened her pace and shortly whispered (a bit loudly), "Here, now. I think that's about done it, for now, don't you, Inga?"

Brune took notice of the servants, then. "Finished, are you? Good enough. Fill our cups and then you are both dismissed. Take some food to the bedroom and get your rest."

Once the two women were on their way up the dark and winding stairs, bowls containing hunks of meat and bread in hand, Inga allowed a quiet sigh of relief to escape the tension in her chest.

Is it worse outside or inside?

Whispers

Raleigh had gone looking for Davis. He wasn't with Reg or in his own room, so Raleigh climbed up the circling stairs and peered into the laboratory. It was dimly lit from magical sources but no one was about.

Next, Raleigh ventured into the small study. Davis wasn't in there, either, but Raliegh had a yen to get acquainted with the contents of the Painted Tower's library. He paused and perused the collections of old tomes. From a cursory inspection, they appeared mostly organized and grouped by subject. Some were grouped by author, however and a couple, bound in maroon-colored leather bore the name and sigil of Clan Talanth. Raleigh felt an excited tingle at the thought one of those might be by the hand of the presumed architect of the tower, Ranius. A book like that would have potential to go a long way toward solving some of Raleigh's personal mysteries and maybe even the immediate dilemma.

He'd devoted his life to unraveling inconsistencies he'd observed in the traditional and written histories of the Great Mage Empire and those inconsistencies were numerous.

Among the magi, there were generally two schools of thought about testing the young into true magehood. Some parents placed their teenaged children into apprenticeships or academies to hone their magical abilities and test their mettle, but there was an ostensibly older tradition many still held to.

The old way was to turn children out on their own around the age of sixteen years. They were expected to test and grow their powers against the wilds of the land and in so-doing, help to tame those very areas in the name of the Empire. Only tested, and proven true magi were permitted back into their hereditary homes, usually years later – if they lived. Those who survived the trials of the wilds still had to defy death once more to finally be proven worthy of their powers, lands and title. The Test of the True Mage, it was called.

Raleigh had been raised with a hybrid of these traditions. He'd spent some time in an academy and some time with an adventuring band of fellow acolytes and the contrast of what he learned through the separate experiences had shaped his skepticism and a burning desire to reconcile the apparent contradictions he'd observed.

Ranius, besides being revered as perhaps the greatest artificer who ever lived, was also the progenitor of clan Talanth – one of the so-called "original" thirteen magi. Anything written by his own hand would be invaluable in Raleigh's personal and perpetual quest for "truth."

The more he reached for it, though, the wider the chasm seemed to grow.

Various historical accounts could not even agree on something as fundamental as the age of the Empire. The official reckoning put the year at 5307, but Raleigh was entirely certain that wasn't accurate. It seemed more like a lie that everyone agreed on.

The narrative of an empire of magi that had stood for over five thousand years reinforced the ideas of infallibility, providence and security. What has always stood always will stand and nothing could possibly threaten it.

Such a story no doubt helps convince the short-memoried peasants that their lords are ordained to eternally be their lords and nothing can be done to change it.

But, the Empire was fractured. The provinces under its sway were strangely divided with wildlands and uncontrolled territories.

If the Empire had really stood, uninterrupted for over five thousand years, how is it that the magi have not managed to knit the Empire's holdings together and control the whole of the continent in all that time?

Raleigh knew better. It was not a well-kept secret. Everyone with open eyes and half a brain knew it was a lie, but it was a powerful one. Even one that many magi took pride in – as if it were historical truth.

Serious scholars and historians used euphemisms to discuss timelines in more accurate terms they understood among themselves without blatantly contradicting the common narrative.

But how long ago was it really, when the original magi founded the first Empire and what became of the thirteenth clan called Tarchis? When did Morticon sink into the Desert of the Dead and the Capitol move east to Bloussen?

There had been a terrible civil war, now known as the Schism, Raleigh knew, but the timelines and circumstances around that remained muddled at best.

Was Ranius still alive when the Schism happened?

Raleigh picked up one of the tomes and turned it over in his hands. It felt warm and smooth. The title on its cover was stamped in with gold foil. "A Treatise on Summoning and Binding"

Whoever wrote it, this is a valuable book, Raleigh knew. He opened the cover and found the author's name on the first page. "By Alista Talanth," it read. With a shrug, Raleigh put the book back in its place and picked up another one.

None of the books there appeared to have been penned by the great Ranius himself and Raleigh didn't find easy answers to the deep and burning questions he shouldered, but in the short time he spent paging through the collection of books authored by his Talanth kin and ancestors, he did at least learn a little more about the nature of the tower and the whisper room. He didn't abandon hope either, that he might find something more concrete about his ancestor, Ranius.

A book like that would probably be kept more securely, somewhere. I'll simply have to ask Davis about it.

With a sigh, Raleigh resumed his search for the master of the tower.

He started back down the stairs and as he was descending past the forth level, spied Davis coming up from below. The elder Talanth stopped on a landing and turned towards the door to the small semi-circular room that was called the Whisper Room.

Raleigh proceeded down the stairs to meet him, but noticed something queer and off-putting about Davis' movements. He was stiff and somewhat erratic. There was a jerkiness to the movement of his joints, almost as if he was a marionette being manipulated by a maladroit puppeteer. Raleigh stopped and observed from several steps above.

The door was locked, it seemed. Davis pushed and pulled and appeared to be exerting himself mightily. He was sweating profusely, as well.

Something is wrong here. Raleigh felt a chill.

It had previously appeared to Raleigh that the tower's many doors simply obeyed the will of Lord Davis and his trusted designees, like Reginald Partha.

Raleigh moved cautiously down a couple steps.

Davis didn't seem to notice him and slammed his hefty old body mightily into the unyielding door.

"Davis?" Raleigh's voice was low and tentative, but he was heard.

Davis wheeled to face him, but looked unsteady. Now, Raleigh could see that Lord Davis' pupils were dilated to a point that his eyes were as black onyx. His hair was matted, his brow pouring sweat down his pallid face.

"Lord Davis? Are you unwell?" Raleigh was nervous. He cast a short protective spell just as the elder Talanth lurched towards him. Raleigh put his hand up before him and Davis suddenly grasped his outstretched forearm. The old man's palm was wet, but also burning hot to a point that the heat of it actually hurt Raleigh's arm.

Raleigh tried to pull away, but the old man's searing grip was surprisingly strong.

Panic was rising and offensive spells came immediately to mind. There was mana in abundance to execute them, but Raleigh did not want to hurt the old Talanth who might have been a great uncle or some-such and had been welcoming and generous to Lana and himself.

The blazing grip on Raleigh tightened, and Davis yanked hard, almost dislocating Raleigh's shoulder as he tumbled forward, his head bouncing off the edge of a cold, reddish stone step.

The round tower starting spinning.

Vision blurred, but with the adrenaline of survival pumping through his veins, Raleigh forced himself back to his feet and turned to face his unexpected assailant.

Davis was on his back, twisted and bent grotesquely across three reddish stone stairs. He laid there motionless, black eyes staring sightless, into the round tower's upper shadows. Traces of blood mixed with oily sweat trickled out from his ear and nose. The skin of his lips was cracked and peeled.

Raleigh stared, mouth agape as his vision started coming back into focus. His head was pounding as he cautiously knelt by Davis. He could still feel heat radiating from the lifeless figure, but there was no sign of breath – no sign of consciousness in his black and unblinking eyes.

Just like Vardan, Raleigh thought, pressing a hand to the side of his throbbing head. *Why wouldn't the door open? What did Davis want with the Whisper Room? I wish I could get in there myself to see.*

The door swung open.

Flickering lights of different colors faintly lit the small, roundish chamber. Peering cautiously from side to side, Raleigh stepped into the Whisper Room.

Near the ceiling, three runes were illuminated by colored lights chasing through their engravings. Red, yellow and purple lights pulsed and flitted. One meant there was a strange presence on the tower's grounds. Another indicated activity connected to the portals in the undercroft – portals that led into the elemental realms. And the third rune, now flashing yellow meant someone was trying to contact the tower's Whisper Room.

Raleigh examined the numerous cubby holes in the wall. Each held a metal rod resembling a large spike, like might be used to anchor a large tent. Beneath those was a stone altar-like fixture with two square basins carved into it. The basins had multiple holes, like drains, but Raleigh realized that they were meant to receive the rods stowed in the cubbies above.

With those rods, Raleigh had no idea where to begin, so he pulled one out at random and examined it. It was a white, shiny metal, about two feet in length and a little over an inch thick. An inscription was engraved along its length. Raleigh couldn't read the script, but he recognized the style. It was the same as the inscriptions on the white stone arches in the undercroft a few stories straight down from the Whisper Room.

It's all one contrivance, Raleigh realized. *The tower, the Whisper Room, the portals — they're all one thing. This whole tower is one great magical device!*

With that revelation, Raleigh also reasoned that the rods and corresponding holes probably weren't strictly for enabling ethereal communication through the Whisper Room.

These could control the entire tower and the portals, below. They might even affect the tower's environs, he thought as he scanned the dozens of cubby holes.

Finding no immediate clue how to make use of the rods, he placed the shining white one back in its place in the wall and turned his attention to the large upturned basin on the opposite wall. It was smooth, crafted from white stone and shaped like a huge bowl, but oddly mounted sideways on the wall. Two rectangular brass plates were set into the wood floor a couple feet from the large dish-shape.

Stand here?

Raleigh tentatively placed his left foot on the left brass rectangle. He stood with one foot on the plate for a moment and observed no changes. The lights near the ceiling continued flickering, lighting the room in queerly swirling colors.

He put his right foot on the other plate and felt a jolt, like a powerful discharge of static energy shot through him — up one leg, to his head, down his torso and out the other leg. He jumped back, startled, but unharmed.

He stepped cautiously onto the brass plates again and when he felt the same shock charge through his body, he was braced for it.

Then, the whispers came to him — whispers that were shouting and full of power and menace. Whispers that were close.

The flesh on Raleigh's arms and neck crawled, his hair stood up. It sounded like a terrible and angry beast was standing right in front of him — right where the big, upturned white basin was.

"Abandon this structure, filthy mortals, and I, the great Grashnuk will make the end of your puny lives quick! This is my promise," the whispers roared.

Raleigh was stunned and his heart was pounding. He could feel the power of Grashnuk through his unearthly and disembodied voice and it was terrifying. It was beyond the aura of any mortal mage Raleigh had ever encountered.

Raleigh's mouth fell open, but he was at a loss to speak back. He felt like he was frozen in place.

"Defy my will, mageborn, and your deaths will linger long in torment you can't yet imagine," the whisper shrieked.

"Great Grashnuk," Raleigh spoke when he'd regained some of his rattled composure, "what do you want with our realm? This tower was erected by my ancestors in accord with pacts made with the spirits of the three realms. Was it you? Did you kill Davis Talanth, who was the sovereign master of this tower?"

"I do not recognize your master's sovereignty, nor the ridiculous pacts you speak of. This realm is mine now. Obey me, mageborn mortal. Open your doors and surrender this structure now. This is your final warning before I smash your walls to dust and strip your feeble flesh apart fiber by fiber," came the horrible, screaming whispers.

Raleigh could feel sweat breaking out on his hot skin. He was duly terrified, but determined to gather as much information from the unprecedented conversation as possible.

Shaking, head and heart pounding and voice wavering, he said back, "What did you do to Davis Talanth? He was my kin. You had no right."

A high, fluttering, roaring sound that might have been laughter assailed Raleigh's ears. "Are you so ignorant to believe the magics you mageborn have used to imprison and enslave my kind only work one way, mortal? I seized your tower's master and the other one before him with *my* magic, but I underestimate the frailty of your kind. Your mortal bodies burn out too easily." There was a pause. "Your fate will be much worse if you fail to obey me! Surrender this structure. Surrender this structure now, to Grashnuk!"

"What incentive do you offer to surrender the tower? You've already said you'll kill us regardless. Mighty Grashnuk, I must say, I'm duly impressed by your power, but I'm not so keen on your negotiating skills."

"I know your kind's aversion to pain. I can make a lifetime of agony for you!"

Raleigh had found his voice and his righteous indignation in speaking back to the creature. "And who are you to undo the pacts of our elders? Your claims are not valid, Grashnuk. Perhaps there is some other bargain we could strike, if I understood your true aims?"

"What need have I of bargains with mortals? I AM DONE SPEAKING WITH YOU, FILTHY MAGE-WORM! Surrender this edifice, or through me, you will discover a new understanding of suffering!"

Raleigh winced against the whispering, screaming onslaught of words and palpable rage as he stepped back away from the metal plates in the floor.

Contact with Grashnuk was broken. Except for the regular claps of thunder dulled by the tower's thick stone walls, the room fell silent.

Raleigh saw that during his otherworldly communion, the door to the Whisper Room had closed of its own volition, but now that he considered leaving the room, it swung open again at his merest thought.

The Length of Nights

The mood among the survivors in the tower was lower than ever after Raleigh had told everyone about Grashnuk's demands and what had become of Davis, but something of a routine had set in.

The storm continued unabated. It worsened, perhaps, but no one attempted to venture outside and the structure remained secure in the days that followed. They still lived. Because of that, there was developing a tenuous sense of safety within the tower's stone walls.

Reg had worked himself out of his bed and was gingerly managing to get around the tower on a pair of old crutches. He was dutiful, despite his injuries and did his best to pitch in.

The magi had taken to sleeping in shifts to ensure the tower was always under watch and everyone within contributed to their collective security.

Raleigh, when he wasn't making rounds double-checking the tower's entry points, availed himself of the library. Gavin occasionally paced around the small study room himself, paging through an odd tome or two, but Raleigh was mostly left to himself, there.

Brune had shown some interest in Vardan's laboratory and spent a little time alone in there getting acquainted with its contents.

Tanya and Inga continued to prepare meals and took care of the washing up after, but had little else to do. Their masters grew increasingly restless, their conversations, curt.

"It appears to me that young Raleigh Talanth has become the de facto lord of the tower," Gavin said one night as he sat at the kitchen table with Brune.

As usual, their servants busied themselves preparing the next meal and pretending not to listen to their masters' conversation.

"That seems certain," Brune replied, locking his blue eyes on his elder brother. "He is Davis' kin – even if they weren't closely related. These are Talanth holdings."

"No. I mean more than that." Gavin said. Whatever magic is about this tower – I believe it's come under Raleigh's control. Or, at least partly."

"Yes."

"The doors, for example. The Whisper Room. It's locked securely – but Raleigh seems able to enter as he wishes. Reginald may still hold some sway, but I'd wager Raleigh's will takes precedence, now."

Brune nodded. "There's powerful magic about this tower. Some of it is ancient and unfamiliar, but I've sensed what you're detecting. I believe you're right. Raleigh is the master here, now."

"It's unfortunate, because I think young Reginald Partha would be a more cooperative steward." Gavin said. "But it seems that Raleigh has become the key to communicating with the outside."

"He's made clear that he doesn't favor using the Whisper Room," Brune reminded.

"I don't care what he favors," Gavin snapped. "He must see reason. Who knows how much longer this supernatural storm will keep us all trapped in here."

"I told you, brother. This clan meeting isn't going to be your last opportunity to present your case."

"And I told you that it may well be! We're in increasing danger the longer we are delayed. And besides clan business, we can't stay here in this damned tower forever! We'll soon run out of food and then what?"

"There's food enough for now," Raleigh's voice interjected from the kitchen's doorway.

Startled, Gavin turned around to see Raleigh standing behind him. Brune, smirking, had already seen him coming down the stairway.

"For how long? For how long, Talanth? Tanya, take inventory. Find out how many days of food remain to us. Check the storage room," Gavin ordered.

"Yes, my lord," Tanya said and she started towards the door.

"Wait. Do it after you're done with dinner," Gavin snapped, waving his hand towards the kitchen's hearth.

"Davis believed that the tower's magic will ultimately repel the forces gathering outside – that they can't sustain this intrusion into our plane of existence. They will weaken. The storm will abate." Raleigh said. "There's food enough for now. Waiting this out seems to me the most prudent course with the information we have. We can weather this storm."

"You've been able to make use of the Whisper Room already," Gavin said. "You said it's how the elemental being spoke to you. Surely you can use it again to summon help from the capitol. If I could speak with the Highmage, he could reach my clan's elders on Embassy Row. They would come for us."

"Simply because the elemental spirit, Grashnuk was able to speak to me – to threaten me in fairly dire terms, I might add – doesn't mean that I know how to utilize the Whisper Room. I've been looking for clues in the library, but so far, I'm no wiser on its workings. However, I do believe that the Whisper Room may be connected to the magic of the entire tower, *including* the power that's keeping the portals beneath us *closed*. I think it would be foolhardy to meddle with that without a very firm understanding of it."

Brune regarded Raleigh thoughtfully while Gavin just turned away from him looking scornful.

"We'll figure this out. Together. We'll all get out of here, safe, but we must be careful. The most important thing is that nobody – *nobody* – goes outside. We must not unseal any egress. Opening any door or window invites death in."

Brune and Gavin nodded. They agreed on that much.

"Well, I don't suppose there's any stew or roast venison ready?" Raleigh put his hands on his hips and turned to the servant girls with a hopeful look.

"Not just yet, my lord," Tanya answered.

"There's hardbread," Inga suggested meekly.

Raleigh just shook his head.

Inga busied herself chopping roots for the evening's stew. "Not too long, my lord," she added.

Raleigh nodded and turned back away into the shadows of the round tower stair.

"He's a smug bastard, isn't he?" Gavin grumbled after he was gone.

"He seems rational to me, brother. Be patient."

"You. You're even worse." A stray tear slipped from Gavin's watery eye and slid down his sallow cheek.

A Prince, Named

The ad hoc routine carried on. The magi slept in shifts to maintain vigilance over the tower's security. The servants cooked and cleaned and worried and slept when they could.

When not making his frequent rounds of the tower's doors, windows and portals, Raleigh spent most of his remaining waking time in the library.

On this night, again, Lana found him there, seated beside a small table, a stack of old tomes at his elbow and one in his lap.

Is it night?

It was had to keep track of the time of day or even what day it was with staggered sleep schedules and stormy skies as dark as midnight at all times. The sun hadn't breached the heavy black clouds for nearly a week.

"You never joined us for dinner," Lana said.

Raleigh looked up from his reading.

"Here. Tanya sent me with a bowl for you."

Raleigh closed the book. "This one's an interesting treatise on the elemental spirits of the sky." he tapped the cover before setting it on the stack beside him. He accepted the bowl of warm stew from Lana.

"Anything useful?" Lana sat down in a chair opposite Raleigh's.

"Well, yes. Very, I think. I found mention of Grashnuk, in fact."

"Really?" Lana's interest was piqued. "Our elemental friend is important enough to be mentioned by name, huh?"

"Very very important." Raleigh touched a spoonful of the stew to his lips and found it not too hot. He swallowed a bite, then stirred his bowl absently as he continued. "I'm afraid we're dealing with an exceptionally powerful being. No ordinary elemental, but a prince of them, it appears."

"Oh."

"Yes. Oh. He's noted as the first son of the king of the winds and he's noted as well as being rather troublesome."

"Troublesome. How?" Lana started. "Well, he's certainly trouble for us!"

"It doesn't go into great detail, but specifically, it says he's rebellious."

"Rebellious against whom?"

"In context, against his father the king, I believe. I still have to read further."

Lana nodded. "If there is anything I can do to help…"

"Just keep looking for any books about the tower itself, or its creator."

"Ranius."

"Ranius. I'm assuming so, anyhow." Raleigh took another spoonful. "Not as good as last night," he observed, putting the spoon back in the bowl.

"Not as hot," Lana suggested. "Your bowl had been set aside for a while."

Raleigh shrugged faintly.

"Hear any further grumblings from our DeVon friends?"

"Certainly," Lana replied. "Gavin was going on about the Whisper Room again," she began.

Raleigh looked up.

"He's convinced that you have dominion over it – and the whole tower, for that matter and he seems rather hard boiled in resentment," Lana went on.

"Because I won't open the door for him to study it himself," Raleigh concluded for her.

She nodded.

"He's right, about something, though. Since Davis died, the tower must recognize me as his heir. It obeys my will, sometimes before I even realize what I want. Doors and locks, at least. I sense its power in a new way, but I don't yet understand the scope of its capability."

"Have you talked to Reg about that?"

"A little. He had been granted some degree of control over the tower by Davis and he retains that, but it's only menial. Beyond opening doors, Reg wasn't let in on much."

Lana tapped a second pile of books that were at her elbow on the small table. "These ones looked interesting," she said. "Have you had a chance to peruse them for clues?"

"I've been caught up in trying to understand the powers that assail us. I paged through a couple of those, though. There's interesting lore, here, but about the tower, specifically, there's precious little. At least that I've seen so far."

"I'll keep looking." Lana got up and moved towards one of several bookcases.

"There are some spells here I've a mind to learn," she said, pulling one book off the shelf. "Later, of course. Now's not really the time for it."

Raleigh frowned, putting his spoon back in the bowl and setting it aside.

"Something wrong?" Lana noticed Raleigh looked extremely fatigued, just then.

"What I'm looking for might not even exist," Raleigh said with a sigh and rubbing his eyes. "I feel so sleepy."

"Yeah. You've been in here reading all night," Lana said, turning back to the rows of books. "Did you even sleep?"

"Yes," he replied after a moment. "I slept... perhaps not enough. I feel... I feel unwell. I think I need to go lie..."

There was a shuffling clamor and a loud bang.

Lana whirled to find that Raleigh had fallen out of his chair and collapsed in a heap on the hard wooden floor.

Dark Deeds

Reg sat on the library floor. "I know this toxin," he said after he'd examined Raleigh's unconscious body. "Blue lips and fingertips, quickly feinting and then comatose sleep… This is ketaxis. I've seen it happen to Vardan. This is bad. This is very bad. Very very bad. How did this happen? Was he in the laboratory?"

"Well, yes. Probably, but mostly just here in the library. What is it? Is it deadly?" Lana was near panic.

"Oh, yes," Reg said somberly. "Quite deadly. Vardan nearly died from exposure. He uses the chemical for certain material refinements and transmutations – used, I mean. He used it often in his alchemical work and he knew the dangers, so he usually kept a store of an effective antidote in the laboratory. A very powerful antitoxin."

Lana brightened. "Oh! Great. Where? What does it look like? I'll go fetch it!"

Reg shook his head. "He used it all up – when Vardan poisoned himself by his own hand – it wasn't that long ago. He used his supply of the antidote up."

"What is it?"

"It's a natural remedy, actually. A kind of rare fungus. He cultivated it himself, too."

"Oh, good. Where? There must be more." Lana was growing frantic. She put her hand to Raleigh's neck to feel his breathing and pulse. His breath was shallow, his pulse rapid.

Reg gave Lana a look that was less than inspiring. "Vardan grew the fungus in a cave beneath the bridge. Out there…" He pointed vaguely to the north side of the tower. "I'd simply go harvest some, but with the storm and my legs…"

"I'll go," Lana said. "Tell me where to go and what to look for and I'll go."

Reg shook his head. "No one should go out there. It's certain death."

"I survived for days out there before Raleigh saved me and led me to your tower. I can do it again." She grit her teeth. "If I must."

Reg shook his head again, but said, "The cave is used for storage and once housed a dungeon. It was exposed long ago when part of the butte this tower stands on collapsed. So, that stone bridge was built to span the chasm. The cave entrance is directly beneath the bridge. There are two cave entrances, actually. One on either side of the chasm, but the one you will be interested in is on the south side, towards the tower. Look. I don't think this is a good idea. Raleigh himself said we should not so much as crack a window."

"Reg, he saved my life and I'll do the same for him. Of course I will. Tell me more."

"At the end of a natural passage, there is a gate. The gate requires a key." Reg pulled a key on a chain out from his red robes. "This key. But, there's more. The gate is guarded by a bound spirit. No one may pass except those the spirit knows or those who have the secret phrase."

"What is the phrase?"

"When challenged, you must say to it, 'you're just some dead thing.'"

"You're just some dead thing."

"Yes. Say that and it should let you pass."

"*Should?*"

"Well, so I'm given to understand."

Lana sighed deeply.

"Once through the gate, there is a passage to the right that leads into a round chamber. The fungus grows all over in there. It's somewhat luminescent. You'll see a faint green glow. A handful of it is enough. Find a clean bag or cloth in the laboratory to carry it back. You'll have to be quick. In an hour or less, I'm afraid, Raleigh will be stiff and dead. Ketaxis poisoning kills fairly quickly."

Lana searched Raleigh's pockets and pouches for anything that could be useful and got more details from Reg before she made her way down to the tower's front entrance and donned her black cloak.

Into the Dark

Bracing herself, Lana stepped out into the cold, black, stormy night. Lightning flashed, the rains poured down and the wind snapped the folds of her black cloak as she sloshed, already soaked and miserable, across the flooded flagstones. Behind her, the great door greedily closed away the warm glow within the tower.

Lana had packed Raleigh's light sphere in her pouch, but its gleam was meager for the conditions and she didn't want anything to draw attention to herself out there. Still, she could roughly follow the terrain by the frequent flashes from the sky.

She made her way carefully around the tower grounds and out towards the slope, some hundred yards to the south. From there, she peered down into the blackness of the canyon. She couldn't see it, but could hear the roiling water crashing around the bend in the river, mixed with the din of the raging storm.

Reg had told her about a switchback trail down the steep incline that would provide the surest footing, but Lana couldn't see where it began in the dark, so, taking a guess, she proceeded slowly, cautiously down the slick, muddy hill.

I should come upon it eventually, she figured.

Lana lost her footing a couple times, falling back onto her rear into the sucking mud, but she struggled back to her feet and carried on, inch by inch down into the canyon.

If it were someone other than Raleigh, would I even still be out here doing this? She thought, somewhat ruefully. *He saved my life.*

Determination bucked up, she increased her speed slightly and that proved imprudent when she kicked into a large but unseen rock, tripping over it, bashing her shin hard on the jagged stone and planting her face straight into the freezing, but viscous mud.

She couldn't have cried out if she'd wanted to, face submerged in liquefied earth. She'd tried to stop her fall before her head hit the ground, of course, so her hands were also mired, deep in the muck.

Her shin on fire and the wind knocked out of her, she tried to rise but could not; tried to roll over, but could not. Nose and mouth sunk into the mud, she couldn't breathe.

Panic set in.

Lana thrashed and struggled and managed to get her face out of the ground.

She cried out in pain and frustration. And regretted it.

I can't be calling attention to myself, she chastised herself as she worked her way into a seated position in the morass, face turned into the wind and rain, wiping the mud from her eyes.

Lana's shin was throbbing under her water-laden hose and robes. Feeling around it, she could already tell it was swelling, but wasn't broken.

She forced herself back to her feet and limping, slogging, slowly and painfully, she continued to descend.

After a time she couldn't have pinpointed, Lana came upon a portion of the trail Reg had mentioned. It was covered in crushed stone and relatively level compared to the rest of the incline she'd been laboring down. When the lightning flashed, she could see its dark path before her. With some degree of relief, she limped along the trail until it turned back the other way, cutting diagonally across the slope. Despite Lana's fresh limp, the way down became much easier.

There was some small shelter from the wind as she descended deeper into the canyon and though the storm was terrible, it was no where near as dangerous as the supernatural tempest at the center of it all. That tempest, flashing red and purple lightning and hurling debris hard and fast enough to take a person's head off, as far as Lana knew, still blocked escape from these broken lands back the way she and her doomed companions had come.

Though all the members of her band had come from different clans, she had developed a sense of kinship with them. They had been though a lot. They'd survived a number of perilous adventures by relying on one another. Now they were all gone. Lana still didn't fully grasp that reality. She'd been too focused on simple survival to grieve and accept that she'd never see Daxos D'Normic, Osmund Lazarian or Arvin Happ again. Arvin, she was only mostly certain of. She'd seen the other two die with her own eyes. The purple-robed young Happ had been ever the optimist, though.

Arvin would hold out hope, Lana imagined as she pressed on. *Perhaps he's found shelter out there, somewhere.*

Lana's right leg burned with every step from the stone she'd tripped over and suddenly, pain flashed through her left leg as well.

She'd not seen or heard the dark creature with jaws full of needle-like teeth that clamped around her calf.

The constant rain and muddy, flooded earth near the river had made good conditions for the black river eels to slither ashore and Lana had drawn their attention by crying out.

The first strike was just to test their prey and the large snake-like fish found Lana a vulnerable target. Others – many others –

around her, their almost human eyes flashing brilliant blue in the lightning, moved in for their share of the warm-blooded feast.

Lana had a dagger on her belt, but she had access to something even keener. Energy flowed around the vicinity of the tower – energy she could use. Though physically battered, her magic was strong again. Strong for a novice like herself, anyhow.

She drew magic into herself and invoked the mental patterns to cast her spell. Lana's aura became charged, crackling with visible power like the lightning streaking through the clouds all around. When the eels struck en masse, they were flung back by a mighty shock, scorched and lifeless or deathly wounded, slapping into the mud.

Lana quickly accessed her surroundings and found her spell had been quite effective, but the very atmosphere seemed to change after she cast it. The sound of the wind altered noticeably and ominously. Its tone, a forlorn howl. Her spell had invoked the elemental air and it seemed as if some power had taken notice.

A couple of the creatures had survived, though most were either dead or rendered harmless for the moment. The first eel that had attacked Lana was still attached excruciatingly to her left leg, however. She drew her dagger and plunged it into the blue-eyed creature's head, which stopped its thrashing, though its numerous long teeth still pierced her flesh.

The eerie howling of the shifting winds unsettled the young Arcana. It began to sound angry.

Lana took Raleigh's luminance sphere from her pouch to better ascertain if any of the eels were still slithering around the dark muck in her vicinity and she saw one still moving towards her.

She'd first thought to burn it, but the nearest fire element was inside the tower and too far away for her to channel. Air and water, she had in abundance, she realized. With a gesture guiding a burst of magic power, she froze the considerable volume of water around the eel in an instant, trapping it in ice. Her dagger finished the job just as the wind's intensity increased, almost knocking her over.

Determining the immediate threat was dealt with, Lana could turn her attention to extracting the dead eel's teeth from her calf. She knew she was bleeding – probably a lot, but couldn't tend it well out in the black torrent of rain.

Tossing the eel carcass angrily aside, she determined to deal with her leg once in the shelter of the cave she sought.

She advanced, slowly, painfully, miserably to the shore of the river. The wind was angry whispers and brutish howls as it assailed Lana on her path.

The south side of the butte she'd descended was sloped, but the rest of the way around was sheer and unscalable, except where a part of the land bridge had collapsed some untold centuries past, forming a chasm. The rubble at the bottom of that chasm formed a slope towards the river on the east side of the butte making it possible to climb up to where some caves had been exposed in the collapse.

A man-made stone bridge now spanned the gap in the earth above. It was the same bridge Lana and Raleigh had crossed to reach the lonely tower in the storm. Lana had to get up to the caves under that bridge.

Reg had said there's usually a narrow beach that's traverseable from the river landing around to the gap, but with the constant storm, the roiling river had swelled and overtaken all dry land around the east side of the butte. Lana was forced to wade through a treacherous and freezing current.

"I almost wish Raleigh hadn't saved my life," Lana muttered miserably as she slogged through the muck, in rushing water up to her knees. She knew there were sure to be more eels about and she'd never see them coming from below the water. She kept her dagger in hand as she made her way around.

She considered casting her shocking spell blindly into the water before her, certain some peril lurked below the roiling surface. She worried that it could splash back onto herself if there was nothing there but water, though.

Something beneath the dark surface brushed her leg and she jumped back, kicking that leg reflexively and she fell into the frigid and rushing waters. Splashing and thrashing, she got clumsily back to her feet and hurried her pace, sloshing as fast as her burning legs would carry her through the shallows of the overflowing river.

At last, she came upon the great crack in the butte's natural causeway. It was about forty feet wide and a rocky slope rose up from the river into darkness above. When the lightning flashed, Lana could make out the narrow silhouette of the bridge spanning the chasm far above. When she and Raleigh had crossed that bridge not long ago it had been in hope of finding shelter and safety.

This is not that!

She was relieved to be out of the dark water, but both legs were ablaze with pain. She was losing blood, freezing cold and soaked to her bones as Lana climbed the slick rocks. Water was cascading down the muddy slope almost like a waterfall and stones slipped out from under her as she went.

She bashed knuckles, knees and shins, tore her black robes, scraped her elbows, but she pressed on, almost numb to it by the time she reached the mouths of two caves, one on each side of the slope, leading into the rock formation upon which the Painted Tower was built.

The natural tunnels were used by residents of the tower for storage of certain goods and they contained the antidote Lana sought. A luminescent fungus that Lord Vardan made sure to cultivate in case his transmutations went awry.

She briefly wondered what might be in the other one, but the cavern to her left was where Reg had directed her. She produced the luminance sphere and entered, dagger still clenched in her other hand. The natural shape of the cave had been modified over the years and needlessly ornate arched braces shored up its stability here and there. The floor was fairly level and became mostly dry about twenty feet inside.

Relieved to be sheltered from the brutal elements and every other terrible thing outside, Lana set down the sphere and dagger and heaved up her robes and leggings for a look at the damage the eel had inflicted. Fresh blood still streamed out from a dozen puncture wounds all around her calf and shin.

Are those slimy devils poisonous?

She thought she remembered hearing something about river eels being toxic, but she wasn't sure if they were venomous or just poisonous to eat. It would be ironic if she ended up poisoned while trying to get an antidote for Raleigh.

Nothing to do about it now. Maybe Vardan's antitoxin work's on eel venom, too, she thought. She doubted it, though.

Lana cut some black cloth away from her sopping robes to tie bandages around her leg and deemed it the best care she could manage with what little time she had to get back to Raleigh.

Grateful for respite from the punishing rain and wind, she pushed herself gingerly back onto her feet, picked up the sphere and dagger and shuffled on, deeper into the cave.

Shivering as she limped along, she cast a minor spell to chase away some of the chill in her bones.

The passage opened into a larger, irregular chamber. Iron bars divided the cavern. They glowed with a blue energy that Lana's mageborn eyes could perceive in the darkness. A gate adorned with curious metal glyphs was set in the middle. There were some crates and iron boxes stowed beyond the bars and the barely perceptible shape of a white stone arch against the far wall. Reg had provided a key for the gate, which Lana fished out from her pouch.

"Stop." A deep voice, source unseen echoed off the rock.

Startled, Lana took a step back and looked all around the chamber, sensing no other presence.

"Who are you?" The deep voice intoned.

"I'm Lana, sent by Reginald Partha," she said, remembering what Reg had said about the magic guardian. "You are just some dead thing," she recited, as Reg had instructed.

Lana sensed, more than heard a sigh. "You may pass," came the fading voice.

Tentatively, Lana stepped up to the rusty gate and put the key in the lock. It screeched and resisted, but yielded to some force.

Beyond the gate, two smaller passages led roughly southward out of the chamber. There was also an odd stone arch, but that looked to be purely decorative. It was neither doorway nor support structure. Set against a flat, reddish stone wall at the back of the cave, the smooth, seamless white stone arch arch was carved with wispy symbols that Lana didn't recognize.

Lana took the right passage, per Reg's instructions and she came into a craggy, roughly circular chamber that glowed with a soft green light. Here, walls, ceiling, stalagmites and patches of the floor were covered in luminescent fungi that resembled tiny mushrooms.

At last!

Using her dagger, Lana harvested a couple handfuls of the fungus into her pouch.

We're even after this, Raleigh... In fact, you might owe me one.

The object of her mission obtained, Lana made haste back to the cave entrance and, bracing herself, stepped back out into the storm. Feeling accomplished, she was more energized as she descended the rocky slope in the gorge and made it back to the river. She waded around the butte, eyes scanning for eels or other dangers, and finally trudged onto the shore at the south face of the butte.

"Now all I have to do is go back the way I came, but *up* the big damn muddy hill, instead." Lana said to herself with a sigh, scanning the black muck for any sign of movement.

Nothing further molested her on her way back up the slope to the tower. Nothing except the slippery mud, heavy rain and blasting winds, that is. Winds with a voice that was becoming increasingly distinct, if Lana wasn't losing her mind. She didn't recognize the language, but the shouting whispers of the raging storm were beginning to sound almost human.

Limping, bleeding and exhausted, Lana grimly pressed on, imbued with determination. She'd obtained the antidote – now she just had to get it to Raleigh.

Lightning flashed, setting the tower in silhouette against the electrified sky.

It's not that far, Lana thought, but now having to struggle up the slippery slope with muddy water cascading down, it seemed much farther than it first appeared. Half limping and half crawling, she slowly ascended the butte.

Her right leg slipped out from under her and her knee came down hard on a jagged stone protruding from the earth adding injury to injury. She fell forward into the muddy ground, but kept going forward by crawling, desperately grabbing fistfuls of mud until she came upon the semi-paved switchback trail that would make the going slightly easier.

Then, over the din of punishing rain and wind and thunder, a new sound arose from behind her and Lana spun around to see the cause of the squelching, gurgling and moaning noises.

Only sporadically illuminated by the flashes of lightning, four human-like figures appeared to be clawing their way up out of the muck. Dripping and covered in dark mud, they rose up from the sopping ground. Covered in mud? No. They were made of the stuff, Lana realized. These were creatures of elemental earth.

She'd been frozen in place, captivated by their bizarre appearance, but Lana regained her senses as she glanced back up towards the welcoming light of the tower. She got back to her feet on the crushed rock of the trail and broke into a staggered run, as the moans of the mudmen at her back grew louder and angrier.

Finally, as she neared the structure, the paved path immediately in front provided some relief from the sucking mud.

She splashed across the flooded flagstones and she saw the great door draw open, beckoning Lana back into its warm yellow glow.

She was even more grateful for the sight of that yellow warmth than the first time she'd approached the tower. That provided the impetus for a renewed push and after a quick glance back at the mudmen who were fast closing the distance between them, she increased her speed, forcing the pain away for the sake of pure, animal survival.

None too soon, Lana bolted though the doorway and stopped, holding herself up against the wooden wall of the entryway to watch the massive tower door begin to scrape shut behind her. She slumped to the floor in a soaking black puddle of relief and exhaustion.

She shuffled to the divan and sat to rest before the blazing hearth a moment. The tower door's final thud was a promise of sorts – of some level of comfort and security within the thick stone walls. Lana didn't fail to notice the perimeter runes near the ceiling flickering with an urgent reddish light, but she was hopeful that the mudmen would not be able to get through the tower's wards.

There was no time to rest, yet. With effort, Lana heaved her reluctant body, protesting, up off the divan. She dropped her heavy, rain and mud-sodden cloak on the floor behind her and shuffled towards the main stair, leaving a trail of dirty water and blood as she went.

Within the Glow

Lana limped her way up the round tower stairs and suddenly heard raised voices as she neared the kitchen.

"No. I don't consider the matter at all settled," Reg said, loudly.

"I am ashamed and embarrassed. Mortified, even. But as unthinkable as it is, the evidence is undeniable," Gavin said. "My own servant!"

Lana stepped gingerly into the kitchen.

"It is unbelievable," Brune was more calm in his agreement.

Inga stood stiffly in the corner, as far from the magi as she could remove herself and, seeming petrified, also appeared to be desperately, but not altogether fruitlessly, attempting to invoke the power of invisibility. The pity was, she had no such power.

Tanya was nowhere to be seen.

"Where is Raleigh?" Lana interrupted.

Everyone turned to take in the soaking, black-robed, blonde waif in the kitchen doorway. They were all clearly surprised to see her. Even Reg – who had sent her out on her desperate mission – regarded her with widened eyes.

I must be quite a sight.

"We moved the poor lad to his bed," Brune said after a moment.

"Did you get it?" Reg asked.

Lana nodded emphatically. "In our usual room?"

"Yes. And there might be someone else who needs it," Reg replied. "How much did you get?"

"A lot. Enough, I think. More than enough. There's no time to waste." Lana turned towards the winding stairs that led to the guest room Reg had provided when she and Raleigh had first arrived at the tower seeking protection from the storm.

"Lana! Wait! They have to be prepared!" Reg called after her, lurching awkwardly forward on his crutches.

Lana stuck her head back into the kitchen. "Oh."

"Inga, a tea cloth, please," Reg called the frozen young servant into action.

She was terrified, but that wasn't necessarily an unusual state for her these days and she did know how to obey. She found a cheesecloth for Reginald, then retreated right back to her corner.

"Here. Put them on the table" Reginald instructed Lana.

She produced the pouch of fungi.

"Spread it out and chop it up, finely." Reg instructed.

Lana chopped up the luminescent mushrooms and Reg tied a handful of the diced fungi into the cheesecloth for steeping. A kettle was already hung over the fire and Reg used that to brew his antidote. He made enough for two cupfuls. "Now, take this to Raleigh," he said urgently, passing one steaming earthenware cup to Lana. "Just get it into him anyway you can. There are funnels in the laboratory if necessary."

Careful not to spill, Lana made haste up the stairs. She didn't even notice the barely-bound wounds on her legs, the to the bone chill, muscle aches or the numerous scrapes and bruises she'd suffered. Raleigh needed her and she was so near to fulfilling her desperate mission.

It was no easy task, getting an unconscious Raleigh to drink the pungent-smelling antitoxin tea, but little by little, it was going down without choking the poor, young Talanth to death.

When the cup was empty, Lana was surprised to find that Gavin had followed her up the stairs and was now standing in the doorway to the guestroom, his hands clasped behind his back.

"You're a faithful friend," Gavin said once Lana noticed him.

Lana, on her knees beside Raleigh's cot, cocked her head.

"I need to apologize for my servant. I feel responsible, but I can't understand why she would do such a terrible thing," Gavin said.

"What do you mean, Lord DeVon?"

"It was Tanya, you see… she poisoned young Raleigh, here. I don't know why. Fear, I suppose. Fear can act strangely on the simple mind of a peasant."

"Tanya? Poisoned?" Lana's mind raced. *If Tanya had indeed poisoned Raleigh, there was no way she acted alone.*

"Reginald, bless his heart. Such a compassionate lad. He made more of that antidote for Tanya, because she managed to poison herself, too. But, I intend to exact swift justice. She'll have no use for the antidote once I slit her throat. Gavin's hands came out from behind him. One held a glinting blade.

Lana was a novice, but even she could detect the aura of magic around the dagger with Gavin framed in the shadows of the doorway. She stood, wincing against the pain. Her battered hands unconsciously balled into small, pale fists.

"It's how we knew it was her, of course. Stupid girl. She seems to have gotten a much smaller dose, but she's definitely fallen ill to the ketaxis, too." Gavin took a step into the small bedroom.

Lana took a step back.

"But, you… Aren't you a dear dear friend? And resourceful? How you surprise me. The heroine of the hour, returned,

98

triumphant with the antidote for poor Raleigh, here and so *undoing* Tanya's dark deed. Wasn't that... unexpected?" Gavin smiled, glanced, through glossy eyes, at the dagger in his hand and took another step.

"I..." words escaped the battered young Arcana.

"Oh, yes. You're a clever one," Gavin breathed. Irritation and menace became all too clear in his voice. He took another step towards Lana, waving his magic dagger in absent little circles.

"Brother." Brune's voice was stern and steady from the shadows of the stairway.

Gavin, a tear sliding down his sallow cheek, was midway through another step into the room, but froze in his tracks.

"What is it, *Brother*?"

"We need to have words. It's urgent." Brune said, coming into the room. He put his hand firmly on Gavin's wrist – the wrist attached to the hand that held his enchanted dagger.

Gavin's rheumy eyes flashed angrily between Lana and his blue-eyed brother. After a moment of consideration and one more look at Raleigh's helpless, prone form, he reluctantly followed Brune out of the room and down the stairs, hissing angry inquiries all the way.

Lana sat on Raleigh's bed and leaned forward as the impossible strength that had been sustaining her suddenly fled her body. She shook uncontrollably and she wept.

A Dark Hand of Magic

"Oh, Tanya, what have you done to us?" Inga murmured as she paced nervously around the small bed chamber that had been provided for the DeVons by the masters of the tower.

The square room had one window set deep in its thick reddish walls. That window was covered with fine silk curtains that did little to block the flickering storm light from outside. The room was otherwise dimly lit by a simple oil lamp on a shelf by the wooden door. The somewhat cramped room was furnished with four modest beds, a couple wooden chairs and a small square table.

Inga was scared. Fear was a part of her daily existence in the tower to some degree or another, but now she felt death was closing in. It was very near.

Tanya, who was only slightly older but far more experienced at serving the magi directly was in a dire predicament and Inga wondered to what extent she'd share her mentor's fate.

Tanya had been restrained by ropes and was bound to one of the wooden chairs. Without the ropes, she'd have fallen to the floor in an instant. She was barely conscious and looked only half-alive.

Gavin had made great theater of accusing her and tying up her limp arms and legs, but no one seemed particularly impressed by his performance. Even if Tanya had poisoned Lord Raleigh, she could have only been Gavin's catspaw, but Inga wasn't sure of even that much.

What she did know for certain was that Tanya and herself were in more danger than ever before.

"I didn't do anything," Tanya croaked weakly.

Inga moved closer and knelt by her bound compeer. "What?"

Tanya struggled for enough air to speak again. "I didn't do anything," she breathed. "I'd never dream to try an' harm a mage lord."

"I believe you," Inga said, looking at her counterpart's face. Tanya's lips were blue, her skin ashen.

"I'd never want to hurt anyone," Tanya labored to add.

Inga put her hand on Tanya's and found it was near cold as ice. She shivered.

Tanya's head lolled and she fell unconscious, but stayed mostly upright, still bound to the chair.

The door opened with a bang and Lord Gavin entered, followed by Lord Brune.

Inga hastily backed away to a corner of the small bedroom.

"I was just..." Gavin began but was cutoff by his younger brother.

"I know what you were just doing," Brune snapped. "Your mad ambitions have completely clouded your senses."

"I'm the elder, here," Gavin pulled himself into a prideful stance.

"You're an old fool," Brune snapped back, blazing blue eyes flashing angrily.

"Now, see, here, brother! We are in a critical situation and I demand..."

"Tenu Senmove!" Brune growled in the language of magic as he raised his hand towards the elder DeVon.

Gavin appeared frozen stiff by his brother's magic, but though unable to move his body, he retained the ability to speak. "How dare you?!"

"No. How dare you? You've attacked a Talanth in his own tower on Talanth lands."

"I've done no such thing! Besides, this isn't Raleigh's tower," Gavin said. "Raleigh is of no consequence at all. Now, release me at once, or..."

"Or what? Go on, Gavin. You're older and more powerful than me. Use your magic and break free."

Tears were streaming down his face as Gavin quietly confessed, "I can't. I think you know I can't."

Brune looked askance at his brother. "I was pretty sure."

"When I saw that bloody ritual of Father's, something happened to me. Some dark magic affected me. I've been accursed."

"You're pathetic, Gavin. A weeping, weakling Trueblood." Brune spit.

"He's performing dark rituals with the blood of our peasants! Drinks it, even – after he's ravaged them..." Gavin's voice wavered. "It's forbidden... heresy, and it's inhuman, besides!"

"Were you traumatized, *brother*? You saw something scary and lost your magic?" Brune sneered. "I'm embarrassed that I ever called you brother. Peasants are plentiful, Gavin. We have thousands of them. You completely miss the significance of what you witnessed."

"You already knew!"

"Yes. Father discovered the secret of immortality – a secret he never meant to share with you. Because you're weak. And you're a traitor, as well," Brune's voice was filled with disgust and loathing, but his blue eyes sparkled mirth and he laughed.

Gavin looked confused as tears leaked down from both sunken eyes.

Inga tried to shrink into the shadows of the little corner she occupied in the small room.

"The best part of all this, Gavin, *brother*, is... and you're going to enjoy this... The best part is that Father knows all about your plot to overthrow him. He always knew. He asked me to go along with you to observe who else you might have turned against him. You were never going to succeed. Lead our clan? A sniveling Trueblood pretender who can't even use his magic? Ha!"

"You've betrayed me?" Gavin seemed sad more than angry as he stood, helpless in the grip of his brother's spell.

"Betrayed? How could I betray you? I was never with you to begin with. Never for a minute. You failed to see that I was always your foe, from the day Father brought me home.

"I intended to go with you to Blousen to see who of our clan might be listening to you, but now you've gone too far and put us in an unacceptable predicament. No one believes your servant poisoned Raleigh and even if she played a role, no one would believe she did it except at your bidding. You'll start a clan war and turn the whole Empire against us, murdering a Talanth in his own tower, where we sought shelter – that was graciously provided!"

Brune turned his head towards his cowering servant, then. "Inga. Go fetch the others. Bring them here."

"My lord?" Inga took a shaky step forward from the dark corner.

"Get Lady Arcana and Lord Partha. Go. Now!" Brune turned back to his brother. "I'll see if I can undo some of the damage you've wrought."

"You'll suffer for this. I swear." They were strong words that Gavin spoke, but they sounded weak – his voice, impotent.

Inga ran off and shortly returned with Lady Lana and Lord Reginald.

"Is there anything else, my lord?" she asked in a quivering voice as she was already sidling back towards the sanctuary of her shadowy little corner.

"Lord Partha, Tanya has been falsely accused and was poisoned by my treacherous brother just as he poisoned Lord Raleigh," Brune said. "Will you use the antitoxin to heal her?"

The red-robed young mage nodded. "Yes. Of course. The cup has already been prepared."

"Inga. Fetch that cup for Tanya. Hurry."

She obeyed and was back swiftly with the second cup of mushroom tea that Lord Partha had prepared.

"She's a murderer. Don't waste your ministrations on that crazed peasant," Gavin said, still petrified from the neck down by Brune's spell.

"No one believes you, brother." Brune said. "Get that antitoxin into Tanya."

Lord Partha helped Inga loosen Tanya's bindings and carefully administered the antidote to her.

"I'm ashamed and embarrassed to admit this, but my brother, Gavin is a traitor to our clan and a would-be murderer as well. It was he who poisoned Lord Raleigh Talanth, of course. He did it because he's in mad pursuit of a conspiracy against our very own father. I was sent to watch him and gather intelligence about the conspiracy, but now that he's tried to murder another mage, I had no choice but to intervene and stop him. He's completely in my power, now."

To demonstrate, Brune made a slight lifting gesture with his hand and Gavin's stiff body raised a few inches off the floor.

"Release me, brother! You'll rue this day," Gavin said through clenched teeth, his feet dangling out the bottom of his brown robes.

"I don't think so, Gavin," Brune replied cooly.

Powerless, suspended and with tears streaming down sallow cheeks, Gavin launched into a tirade of shifting subjects and erratic tacks in a frantic bid to reverse his exhausted fortunes. But, no one seemed at all convinced by his stories or appeals.

He changed to accusations. "It was Brune! Brune poisoned Talanth. I tried to stop him. I would never do such a vile thing. And poison? Poison is a coward's weapon!"

Gavin searched pleadingly from face to face, but his watery eyes could only have seen contempt and obvious disbelief.

Inga was trying her best not to let any emotion show, but she felt mainly fear. Perhaps mixed with a pinch of pity. She tried to look stoic. Tanya was so good at that.

"But, my mission is important. You must understand. My father is a foul creature. An abomination! I did what I had to. You'd all have done the same to save your clans!" The inflection of Gavin's voice turned desperate and imploring.

"You shame us, brother," Brune said. He looked around at the others in the room – looked into their eyes with his brilliant blue orbs.

Inga knew her master saw little but fear in her eyes. She looked away. She looked at the others. Lady Lana and Lord Reginald's eyes were full of contempt, but mixed with some amount of curiosity, she perceived.

Finally, Brune intoned some harsh magical words while raising both his hands toward his floating, adopted brother. "Mortigi forton," he concluded.

The room appeared to darken. An unnatural, cold energy vibrated the air.

"No!!! Arrrgaahh!" Gavin screamed as Brune's spell seemed to drain away what little life was left in him. His head slumped forward as he fell silent.

The others were equally mute. The silence of a tomb oppressed the square stone room as everyone gaped at Gavin's dangling corpse.

"On behalf of Clan DeVon, I apologize for my brother's actions," Brune finally said, breaking the long silence. "The pressing matter of defending this tower remains tantamount and I promise to do everything in my power to aid in our mutual defense." With a gesture, Brune lowered his adopted brother's lifeless body to the floor.

Gavin's lithe form crumpled in a heap of brown robes.

"I did not share in my late brother's over-zealousness," Brune concluded.

Bother

It couldn't be said that Brune DeVon was trusted, and Lana kept careful watch on his activities, but in the end, his help was accepted. What choice had they? There was no mage more powerful left in the tower than he and upon preponderance of the known facts, it appeared that Gavin had likely acted alone in his treachery.

Because it was a fellow clansman who had meted out justice, such as it was, Gavin's death had become an internal matter for the DeVons. It was clan business and far as the laws of the Empire were concerned, the matter was moot.

The antitoxin that Lana had fought so hard to obtain soon proved its worth. It worked almost as fast at reviving Raleigh and Tanya as the ketaxis poisoning had taken them down.

By the end of the day (as best as Lana could judge the time), both Raleigh and the servant girl seemed in decent health.

Raleigh compared his lingering symptoms to having drunk too much. "I think someone slipped a hangover into my mead last night," he had joked while holding his head.

Like Raleigh, Tanya reported throbbing aches in her head and mild nausea, but otherwise seemed well just an hour after she'd been given the antitoxin. Lana could tell that she was also quite traumatized, however. She was noticeably cautious with every word or movement, but also profoundly grateful to have been spared – both from the poison and from her own master's dagger after he'd made clear his intention to execute her.

With his older brother dead, Brune became perhaps even more curmudgeonly, but he participated fully in maintaining vigilance over the tower's security.

Gavin's body was brought up to the laboratory, where he would be embalmed and wrapped for transport back to Devonshire.

There were three cadavers being stored in the tower. Death was pervasive and Lana imagined it as a force unto itself. It surrounded the survivors. It stalked them.

Of course, "Death" had a proper name now. Grashnuk, he was called. An ostensibly rebellious prince of the elemental winds. It was Grashnuk and his allies who were intent on destroying Lana and everyone else still alive in the tower.

According to Raleigh, even surrender wasn't an option, if they wanted to live. Grashnuk had only promised to kill them quickly if they gave up the tower. They'd have to fight if they were to survive.

Again, they slept in shifts that night. Raleigh and Tanya were first to sleep. Brune sat up with Inga in the great hall on the main floor. Lana was well beyond tired and ached from the frayed ends of her long blonde hair to her toenails and Reg was crippled from his fall, but the two of them made their way all the way up the winding stairs to the lookout. Lana brought two cups and a decanter of wine, along with some dried and salted meat.

There was no way of knowing exactly what foods Gavin had contaminated in his scheme to poison Raleigh and his own servant, so, unfortunately, all of the cooked and prepared foods had been disposed of.

The food supply wasn't quite critical, but it was diminished.

By Raleigh's figuring, time was their most crucial resource for surviving the elemental siege on the tower, and it was dwindling while the powerful storm continued unabated.

Reg made a slow circuit of the room, his crutches clicking on the stone floor. He gazed long out the twelve great windows as he went, but there wasn't much to see out there. Rain pounded the glass and the misty parapet walkway that surrounded the lookout.

Lightning burned across the laden cloud strata and that was the primary source of light for Lana and Reg. They kept the room dimly lit with only a low-burning oil lamp so they could better see out into the stormy dark.

Lana sank to the floor, propping her back against the stone wall beneath a massive window. She stretched her legs out and pulled her robes back to examine her injuries. Blood had soaked through her makeshift bandages. She'd not even thought to better tend to herself, so intent was she on delivering the antidote to ailing Raleigh.

Reg stopped his pacing, leaning on his crutches to support his injured legs. "Aren't we a splendid sight, my lady? What happened to your legs? What happened once you got out there?"

Lana rubbed her aching thigh and tipped her head back. "It was not an easy errand you sent me on," she replied. "This leg, I bashed on a rock. Maybe more than one. Feels like maybe *all* the rocks." She pointed at the leaking, bloodied cloth bandages on the other leg. "This one was a snack for a river eel."

"Oh, no." Reg winced.

"The beaches were pretty well flooded, so the eels didn't have much trouble slithering ashore. I dealt with them, but didn't see them coming until one was locked onto my calf. Those bastards have some serious teeth."

"Oh, yes, they do."

"I met your bound spirit in the cave and fortunately, it let me through when I told it what you said to say. That gate could use some oil, though. It was pretty stuck."

"I apologize for that my lady. I know that you did manage, though."

"On the way back to the tower, there was a new menace, too. I don't suppose you can see anything moving around on the ground down there?"

Reg looked out the window again, but shook his head slowly. "I'm afraid not. What was it?"

"Earth elementals, I think. They clawed their way up, right out of all the mud – but it was more like they were made of mud. Tall, dark, dripping creatures roughly shaped like men. I was almost back to the tower by then and I was able to outrun them, thankfully."

Reg scanned the darkness again, then turned back to Lana. "Wait. You did close the gate again, didn't you? In the cave?"

Lana was still as a statue as she considered Reginald's words.

"Lana? Did you lock the gate again after you got the fungus?"

"Well, you didn't say that might be important," Lana began.

"Oh, dear."

"The gate was so hard to move and I was in a hurry – not to mention bleeding. I guess it didn't occur to me that it might be important... To protect some glowing mushrooms."

"Well, did you happen to notice a carving on the wall that looked like a doorway?"

Lana thought about it and nodded, a fresh feeling of dread washing over her. She picked up her cup and took a big swig of wine.

"There's a carving just like it in the undercroft. Lord Davis guessed they're linked magic doors – only none of us knows how to use them," said Reg. "Davis hypothesized that they might work through elemental earth magic."

Lana rubbed her fatigued eyes and shook her head.

"Leaving that carving unprotected could give Grashnuk a way into the tower, if he finds that cave," Reg went on. "Maybe."

"Would Grashnuk know how to use the doorway?"

"I don't know," Reg said softly. "Grashnuk is evidently ancient, and he has shown a proficiency with magic. If I had to guess, I'd say he was probably lurking around these parts when this tower was built. I'd say there's a fair chance he would. And now there are apparently earth elementals, as well..."

"Bother," Lana exclaimed.

Knock, Knock

"I'm very proud of you, Inga."

Inga was stunned. The mix of emotions that shot through her bedraggled being momentarily paralyzed her as effectively as Brune's spell had worked on Gavin.

"You have conducted yourself quite admirably under these trying circumstances," Lord Brune continued.

Her usually stern and stoic master wasn't known for paying compliments.

"Tanya as well," he added.

Once Inga regained her tongue, she curtsied and said simply, "Thank you, my lord."

"Maintain that cool and level head and we'll survive this ordeal. Of course, you will never speak of any of these events to anyone without my explicit instructions to do so."

"No. I certainly won't, my lord."

"Good."

Inga ventured further. "And Tanya, my lord?"

"I said she has done well. It was only my brother who wished her harm – to cover for his own stupid deed. No punishment is due."

Inga was relieved and she felt proud as well. Suddenly, the harrying events that transpired since disembarking from the DeVon's erratic riverboat and climbing up to this strange, storm-besieged tower didn't seem so terrifying. Bone-weary as she was, Inga felt confident for the first time in a long time and that invigorated her.

It was a quirk of the tower's design that the ground floor had no windows. Sitting by the crackling fire in the great hall, one could almost forget the storm raging outside. The tower's colorful and very thick stone walls muted the frequent thunderclaps – but not entirely.

From there, they could see the tower's main entrance, the great metal door at the end of a short wood-paneled entry hall. Above the door were carved three runes.

One of them, they'd been told, would illuminate with magic energy if intruders were about the tower's grounds. That one had been flashing for quite some time with a red streak of light that chased erratically around the stone impression like a fly trapped in a jar.

Inga and her master had made a few trips up to higher levels to look out the windows, but thus far had seen nothing to explain the red lights.

Inga didn't know what the other runes might indicate and if Lord Brune had a guess, he wasn't saying, but all of a sudden, both of those other runes began glowing with blue and yellow energy chasing through their stone-carved shapes.

Then, there came a pounding on the great metal door. The resounding booms were even louder than the storm's incessant thunder.

Brune strode boldly down the wood-paneled corridor towards the door, but stopped as small brownish shapes, like worms began to wriggle under the door.

Not worms, Inga realized. Fingers. Muddy, reddish-brown, grotesquely elongated fingers. They seemed to ooze through the barest crack and reconstitute themselves once inside, but as the fingers pressed in further and began to emerge as entire hands, they erupted in plumes of thick white steam with a loud hissing.

Inhuman shrieks protested from outside and the muddy fingers began to withdraw back under the door, even as they shrank away crackling and steaming.

"The tower's defenses are holding up," Brune observed. "At least for the main door. Let's get back up to where there are windows."

Inga followed her master up the winding stair in the circular tower until they came upon a landing with a window. From there, they they had a line of sight to the tower's main entrance, shrouded in darkness. When the lightning came, they could see the creatures that had gathered outside: tall, dark, dripping beings roughly shaped like men, resolved for a moment in blazing silhouette before the flash.

There were dozens of them that they could see. For all they knew the tower could have been surrounded by dozens more.

"Look, my lord," Inga exclaimed, and Brune looked out where she was pointing.

The flickering storm light revealed several of the mudmen climbing the side of the square tower.

"There are so many of them," Inga whispered, but instantly regretted it. Her master had been proud of her. She had to keep a cool and level head.

Something dark and squishy slapped the window and Inga jumped back from it. Even Lord Brune flinched. It was a muddy hand and soon the mudman's head rose into view as well. Its face, as it were, was mostly featureless, save a vague indentation where human eyes would be and a dark, wet and runny maw that opened wide as the creature regarded them through the window pane.

As they observed each other, Inga began to notice that the mudman was dissolving before their eyes. Separated from the earth, the torrential rain was steadily eroding the creature's form.

The elemental creature slapped its hand against the glass again, but it seemed weaker, sloppier. It was more water than dirt, now. It was shrinking, the mud that formed its physical shape became thinner. The rain was washing it away!

The diminishing creature let go of the wall and fell back to the soaking earth, where they could see it quickly reconstitute itself from the endless supply of mud down on the surface.

"Interesting," Lord DeVon said.

Of Wind and Stardust

When Raleigh woke from the dark waters of troubled sleep, he silently thanked the old goddess, Mishalanthias, who was said to be a healer, but more than that, he thanked the proverbial princes of wisdom. Those old sages of fable had come to Raleigh's dreams with answers.

Raleigh marveled at the power of the unconscious mind to solve problems. Waking with fresh insight, he was imbued with purpose. The poison that had nearly killed him left no trace that he could detect and he was full of renewed energy.

He went straight to the Whisper Room and the door opened for him at his merest thought.

He pulled one of the metal spikes from its cubby in the wall and examined the wispy engraved symbols along its length.

The inscription was not a language Raleigh could read, but elements of it were familiar from the language of magic that he did know. More important than exactly what it said was how it said it. The style of script was identical to the symbols carved on the portal arches down in the tower's undercroft.

Raleigh had earlier guessed that the Whisper Room wasn't a magical device on its own, but rather that it was just a part of a larger system. He postulated that the entire Painted Tower was one great and complex contrivance. "I was right about that. This controls... everything." he spread his hands over the square basins that were full of holes, just the right size to receive the metal rods stored in the wall above it.

"So what does Grashnuk want in here? Control of the portals, control of the barriers between our worlds?," Raleigh muttered. "I don't think his full power is here. Not yet. He's weakened. Maybe that's why he needs the tower's magic – to emerge fully into our world. So, he's brought an army to break in… And eventually, he'll succeed. Probably sooner than later."

Raleigh examined a few more of the rods and saw that they were forged of a variety of metal alloys and were mostly uniform in size, about a foot long, with a wide domed top and a pointed end. They looked quite a bit like huge nails or spikes.

One empty cubby caught his attention. It was bigger and much deeper than the others and it was empty. "I bet that one was important," Raleigh said to himself.

He went around the winding stairs and entered the library. This time, he knew exactly which book he wanted to review. The book one of his ancestors had written about the spirits of the sky, or the wind elementals. He'd found Grashnuk's name in there. "Rebellious" the book called him.

That piece of the puzzle might be the key.

Raleigh picked the book up from a stack on a side table and sat down to read.

He didn't know how much time had passed when he closed the book and set it back on the stack. An hour, maybe two? He'd devoured the old tome, cover to cover.

Raleigh sat in the library chair for a minute, nodding to himself, then, put his hands on his knees and sprang up out of his seat.

He went looking for Lana.

Raleigh found the novice Arcana, sitting on the floor in the dark, but storm-lit lookout room at the top of the tower. Her back was propped against the wall and she didn't acknowledge

Raleigh when he entered the room. Lightning flashed through the great windows from all directions and thunder rumbled, muted through the building's old stones.

"Lana?"

She didn't answer. Raleigh noticed a cup, tipped over near her hand on the floor and alarm started creeping up his chest.

He knelt by her and could see her eyes were closed. He shook her shoulders gently. "Lana!" he repeated more forcefully.

Her head lolled, blonde hair spilling over her face.

"Lana!"

The young Arcana's head bolted back upright and her eyes snapped open. "Yes? Yes. What?" She struggled to focus for a moment. "Oh. Raleigh! How are you?"

"I'm doing very well. *You* should go lie down in a proper bed, though. Look at you. You're beat to hell and exhausted, still trying to keep watch – *and* falling asleep on duty."

"No. I…"

"Listen. I'm going to do something that's going to sound a bit radical, but I need you to trust me."

Lana seemed more alert now, as she listened.

"I'm going to go through one of the portals downstairs. I'm going to enter the sky realm, where Grashnuk comes from."

"What? That's crazy! He'll kill you for certain. The elementals will tear you to shreds!"

"I don't think so. I think I can get help to defeat Grashnuk."

"But you have only just recovered and the creatures out there…"

"I'm feeling better than ever," Raleigh assured her.

"We need everyone to defend against the creatures outside. The mudmen have been trying to scale the tower – they're looking for weaknesses to exploit and hail and lightning bolts have been battering the tower. That's sure to have an impact."

"These creatures outside..." Raleigh repeated, "Look what's been happening *inside*, Lana. Monsters within and monsters without... I fear we're almost out of time, but I've got it figured out." He paused, then restated, "I think I've got it figured out."

"How? What are you going to do?"

"Don't worry. It came to me in a dream."

Lana rolled her eyes and cocked her head. "Oh, well then…"

After Raleigh had seen to it that Lana laid herself down in a proper bed, he made his way stealthily down to the base of the round tower. He intoned the incantation to open the trap door and climbed down into the undercroft.

The room was lit erratically. Crazed patterns of magic light zoomed around the magical inscriptions on the white stone of the arches that marked the portals to the three realms. Beneath one was a shimmer, like waves of heat distorting the air in the Desert of the Dead. His best, studied guess was that one was the portal he sought.

Raleigh held his breath, not knowing what the world of wind elementals would be like for a mortal to enter, and passed under the arch.

The lighting changed.

The walls transformed from reddish stone to a hazy, shifting and flickering blue-gray, but he was still in the undercroft of the tower.

All that seemed unchanged by his passage was the white stone pillar and the three gleaming portal arches that radiated from it.

There was a steady light that seemed to come from everywhere and nowhere at once.

Looking closer at the strange, translucent walls and the arches, he realized he was looking at the storm raging outside the tower, as if the entire structure had turned to foggy glass. Lightning occasionally flashed through eddying mists.

Raleigh realized the tower must be similar to the Cathedral of Fire, in that it existed on the physical and elemental planes simultaneously. The cathedral, once a temple dedicated to gods rarely regarded in modern times had been utterly destroyed in some great battle long ago, but the shape of it still burned endlessly in the Valley of the Battle. Its magical walls still existed on the plane of elemental fire and the raging flame of that realm could be seen, but not felt in the world of men. That great blazing edifice produced no heat or smoke. It was regarded as one of the wonders of the world.

Raleigh tested the apparently insubstantial shape of the stairs and found that the watery, misty shape held his weight as firmly as any stone and he climbed up out of the undercroft.

He explored the strange, transdimensional counterpart to the Painted Tower, but found that it was an empty shell. The semi-transparent structure was identical in shape and layout to the tower he had lately become familiar with, but contained no furnishings or property.

Moving through the empty structure was a little like navigating a maze of mirrors. All the walls, ceilings and floors looked essentially the same, appearing to be made of the same chaos of the shifting elements, wind and water. The tower was the storm.

It seemed to be devoid of people as well as property. That was disquieting to think about and as Raleigh considered it, a brief shiver took him.

They are all right here, in this space, Raleigh realized. *Only slightly displaced into another plane of existence.*

He couldn't perceive Lana or Reg or the others, but he knew they were near – just separated by the thinnest veil between the realms.

The veil is especially thin, here.

Raleigh made his way through the great hall, where he could make out the shape of a cold and empty hearth.

"Brune?" He whispered, imagining that the mysterious younger DeVon was right in front of him. He probably was.

Raleigh half-felt his way along the cool smooth walls until he was moving down the entry hall.

Just like in his own stone and mortar version of the tower, the great main door swept open of its own volition as Raleigh approached.

Outside was nothing but blue sky. Up, down, all around. There was no ground beyond the tower's flickering entryway – none that Raleigh could see, anyhow. He took a tentative step off the translucent and stormy threshold and discovered that there was *something* firm to stand on, even though it could not be seen.

Looking around, at first, it appeared to be an endless and empty plane. There was the stormy, but insubstantial shape of the tower, there was Raleigh and there was nothing else but an infinite blue expanse.

There was light. Raleigh looked at his own hands and they appeared normal, lit as though it was a sunny day, but the light had no source he could discern. No sun blazed in the vast, cloudless sky. No lamps or torches lit the area around the tower.

It's almost as if the air itself glows, Raleigh thought, waving his hands through the still air.

He took a few more cautious steps on the solid nothing beneath his feet before he began a more confident stride.

I'm walking on air.

The problem was that he had no idea which direction to go.

Is there even direction, here? Raleigh could determine which way would be north from the orientation of the tempestuous shape of the Painted Tower behind him, but considered that cardinal directions might have no meaning in this airy realm. The sun rose in the East in his world, but here there was no sun at all.

Where might the denizens of the sky realm dwell? Where do the winds go? Raleigh walked slowly and aimlessly as he pondered.

Beyond the tower, is there even an up or down, here? He was beginning to feel disoriented and suddenly felt a rush in his gut like his was falling. He let out a startled cry.

Looking toward the orientation he perceived as down – towards his feet, anyway, Raleigh could make out a brownish-gray shape.

Wind started rushing up at his face. His maroon robes flapped around him and the brown-gray shape grew larger.

As he continued to fall, he could make out the features of the object he seemed to be falling towards. It was a huge rocky formation, like a mountain in the sky – only the sky was below him, the mountain upside down.

The wind grew louder, whistling past his ears as the mountain loomed nearer, but there was an odd sound to it – almost musical.

"See, it *is* a human," a breathy, but sing-song voice became distinct. It was close. Very close. Whoever had said it was close enough to touch, but Raleigh could see no one. "I told you so."

"That's not a human," whispered another, girlish voice.

"Is so," said a huskier female.

"It's one of the magi. Can't you smell the magic on him?" said the girlish one. That time, the voice was right in his ear and Raleigh flinched.

He continued to fall towards the mountain and the voices matched his velocity, even as they seemed to flit and swirl around him. Raleigh didn't have much time left before he'd be nothing more than a red and maroon stain on a flying mountain in the endless sky.

"Could you help me?" he said.

"Magi *are* humans, stupid," said the first breathy voice.

"Not all of them. Are you an elf, human?" asked the girlish voice.

"How could he be an elf if he is a human?"

"Excuse me, kind spirits, but I seem to be falling to my death! I'd be happy to answer any questions you might have if you could first stop that from happening," Raleigh shouted against the rushing wind.

"We're no spirits, silly elf. We're slyphs," said the breathy sing-song one. "I'm Geshalla."

Raleigh could feel hands gripping at his robes and to his relief, his trajectory towards the mountain slowed.

Raleigh slowed even further and gently, his feet touched down on the surface of the mountain. Once he was steady, the unseen hands released him.

"Only the Landric elves are magi," said the husky voice. "They are green."

Raleigh felt hands tugging at his robes again.

"Really? Are you green under this, elfin mage?" Geshalla asked.

Raleigh pulled away from the slyph's curious hands.

"She means they wear green raiment," said the girlish voice. "This one's robes are not green."

"I'm not a Landric, kind slyphs. My name is Raleigh Talanth."

"Oooh! A Talanth," breathed the husky one. "That's a good name. An important name. This one's important! I'm called Wawasha. I'm honored to make your acquaintance, Raleigh Talanth."

"And I'm called Swish," said the more girlish sounding slyph. "Why have you come here, Talanth mage?"

"I like this one. I think I'll keep him," Geshalla interrupted in her breathy, sing-song voice.

"I… uh… I have come from the tower. I… Uh, what? Keep me?" Raleigh stammered.

The ground, as Raleigh perceived it was fairly level and featureless, but he tripped over some rocky protuberance as he backed away from the disembodied voices of the slyphs. His foot got tangled in his maroon robes and he fell back hard on his tail bone. "Ahhh!" he exclaimed.

"He's a magic user. He probably has many entertaining tricks. He'll make a good pet, I think," came Geshalla's voice from uncomfortably near Raleigh's head.

"I don't do uh…" Raleigh stammered as he struggled back to his feet. "Tricks isn't really what we… Look, I'm on a diplomatic quest."

"You can't just keep magi," said Swish.

"And why not?" Geshalla's voice became indignant. "They capture elemental beings and bind them into all sorts of service, do they not?"

"I need to see the ruler of this realm, actually," Raleigh tried to assert himself with an air of authority as he straightened his robes from his rather undignified and painful fall. "I need to see the king."

"King Ouranos? Whatever for, my pet?" Geshalla patronized.

"I am aggrieved. My people are trapped in that tower." Raleigh vaguely pointed upwards, but the mountain he was on may have been drifting and he had no bearings in this sky realm, anyway. "It's besieged by a wind elemental prince named…"

"Grashnuk!" Wawasha interjected.

"Um, yes. Grashnuk. He's in contravention of ancient pacts, so I've come seeking an audience with the king of this realm."

"I hate that arrogant cur, Grashnuk," Wawasha hissed. "There is his camp!"

Raleigh looked around but couldn't see anything except the blue sky above, below and beyond the floating mountain. There was a cloud that seemed a long way off, but distance was hard to judge in the open sky. "Where?"

"He can't see us so he can't see where you're pointing," Swish said. "He's still tethered."

"I don't see anything. Just a cloud," Raleigh admitted.

"Yes. That's it! The cloud, but you can't see it as it truly is because you are still tethered to your own world. Your perceptions are skewed. You have to break the tether to see things as we see them," Wawasha said.

"I see no tether." Raleigh turned around in a circle, patting all over his body and looking at the ground.

"It's as plain as the tail on a griffin," said Swish.

"How do I break it?"

"You just will it, silly," said Swish.

"Oh, yes. It's easy," said Geshalla. "Go on."

Raleigh closed his eyes and tried to use the skills he'd honed to detect magic auras and force lines and then he could see it. Not with his two hazel eyes, but in his mind's eye, he could see a long shining cord, like silver spun into yarn, behind him and trailing off into infinity.

Once he could see it, he could manipulate it. It was akin to some rudimentary magic – his earliest practical lessons. He broke the tether, essentially by imagining it breaking.

That was simple.

Suddenly, the atmosphere around him changed. It was breezier, cooler and the glowing, golden outlines of three female forms appeared near him on the flying mountain. The three slyphs. They sparkled and seemed to be made of the wind and star dust. One appeared clothed in a shimmering and translucent gown, billowing in a breeze of its own. One was smaller, wore a short skirt and unlike the other two, had wings like a dragonfly. The third looked like a nude woman with long cascading and glinting hair. Her hair was so long and full, as it waved around her, it would almost have preserved her modesty – if she had been possessed of any.

The cloud he'd espied far above became a huge dark tempest, swirling and flashing with myriad colors of lightning.

"That is Grashnuk's camp?" Raleigh pointed at the sinister-looking storm in the distance.

"The part that's in our realm, yes. He's a very wicked prince, so King Ouranos finally banished him – and good riddance – so he's apparently decided to make his new kingdom in your mortal realm. He has followers, though. Grashnuk has gathered an army of elemental spirits and not just of the wind, either. He has allies from the earth and water realms also," Wawasha explained. She wore the long, fluttering and glittering gown.

"He's attacking my realm and the tower that my friends and I have been trapped in," Raleigh explained. "Please, kind slyphs, will you just guide me? How can I find the king?"

"You don't have to worry about that anymore, my pet," Geshalla said. "I'll take care of you from now on." Geshalla was the long-haired female who didn't seem to have any clothes, Raleigh could now see.

"Swish is right. You can't keep him. This one's important," said Wawasha.

"But it's easy. Now that he's broken his tether, it will be even easier to cage him for myself," Geshalla said. "What do humans eat?"

"My lady Geshalla," Raleigh said, "As delightful as your offer sounds, I am duty bound. I must complete my quest. Perhaps I can offer you a bargain for my freedom? I have access to a portal that allows me free travel between my realm and yours. Perhaps there is something you want that I can bring you?"

"A pact?" Geshalla sounded intrigued.

"Yes. A pact," Raleigh said officiously.

"Well, there is something I have always wanted to try," Geshalla said.

"Good. Name it."

"A peach."

"A peach?" Raleigh wasn't sure he'd heard correctly.

"Yes. If you agree to fetch for me a peach, I'll grant your freedom, my pet," Geshalla proclaimed.

"A peach... The fruit?"

"Oh yes. I've always wanted to try one. I've heard of something called a peach pie, too..."

"Do you even eat?"

"Of course. We might not look it to your eyes, but we have bodies just as you and we eat and sleep and make love just as humans do,"

"My lady if you will show me how to find the king of this realm, I will return to you with a dozen peach pies and as many whole peaches as I can carry."

Geshalla sighed. "Very well, mage. We have a pact, but if you break it, I will come and pull all of the pink things right out of your chest."

Fury at the Gates

Hail battered the tower windows and wind howled through the chimneys as the lightning strikes grew nearer and more frequent. Previously occasional claps of thunder had become an incessant rumble that shook the floorboards and furnishings.

The monotonous sound of the bell vibrating in the tower's tallest turret penetrated every room and now a monstrous chanting in some alien tongue was added to the din. Hundreds of inhuman voices repeated the rhythmic mantra and it was loud enough to pierce the thick tower walls and magically reinforced glass.

An undulating yellow glow rose up about the tower and it could be seen from every window, as some magical energy conjured by the elemental beings outside engulfed the Painted Tower.

Lana watched it pulse and waver in the mists through the kitchen window.

Tanya appeared calm as she worked her menial task, peeling potatoes while Inga, more visibly nervous was setting up pots and kettles in the hearth and on the stove.

Brune paced the small room, sometimes stepping out into the stairwell and looking up and down the shadowy steps that wound around the tower wall.

"I can feel the power that's massing against us thrumming in my chest," said Lana.

"That's just a taste of what's coming for us, I fear," said Brune, stepping back into the kitchen. "And just where the blazes are Raleigh and Reginald? We're going to need everyone ready to fight if we're going to survive this siege."

An outstanding clap of thunder exploded above the din of the storm and elemental magic raging outside. The boom shook all the cups and jars in the cupboards as well as the four people in the kitchen. It was the loudest thing Lana had ever heard or felt.

"This tower's magic is strong," Brune observed, "but not invincible. It won't be long before it's breached. But what is the weakest point?"

"The storage room doors," Lana suggested. "Raleigh believed they were added long after the tower was first built."

"Yes. That's a likely point," Brune said thoughtfully.

The fire blazing in the hearth began to flutter. A little at first, but then a lot, as a wind gathered strength, blasting down the chimney. Then, the room was awhirl. Lana's robes snapped to and fro in a sudden gale. Bowls and wooden spoons, cheesecloths, torn drapes and half-peeled potatoes flew and spun around the small kitchen.

Tanya and Inga dove for cover under the sturdy wooden table.

"Estu Malkasita!" Brune shouted, spreading his arms wide and his spell instantly revealed what had been an invisible elemental spirit. It was shaped roughly like a man, but insubstantial, made of shadow with smoke and steam and ash, all whirling around him like a dustdevil. Its movements were as quick as a big cat's.

Before Lana or Brune could even think to cast another spell at the wind spirit, it changed its demeanor, buckling over and staggering back in apparent pain. The steam and smoke that defined its shape began to dissipate in streams shooting out from it in all directions.

The elemental shrieked and flew back into the hearth it had gained entry by. The flying bowls, cloths and utensils fell to the floor with a clatter.

"Did you do that?" Lana asked Brune after she'd regained her breath.

"My spell only revealed it. The tower's magic must have caught up to it, but it got further inside than anything else so far. They are definitely weakening the tower's defenses. It won't be long before we're fighting everything that's out there, because it will be in here with us," Brune pointed toward the bare window, where the yellow glow without had intensified.

"I'm only a novice," Lana said. "My magic is no match for what's out there."

"And neither is mine," Brune said grimly, "At least not for long. Where is blasted Raleigh? He's not as powerful as me, but even his magic could probably buy us a few more minutes, at least."

"Raleigh..." Lana was pretty sure Brune wasn't going to like what he was about to hear. "Raleigh went through the portal," she said softly.

"He what?"

"He was convinced that he'd found a solution to our quandary up in the library and he said that it was on the other side of the portal in the sky realm."

"What solution did he say he'd obtain in the very home of our enemy?"

"He, um. He didn't. He just said I had to trust him. And I do. I just... I just hope he's quick about it."

"For all our sake, so do I," Brune hissed. "Where is Partha, then?"

"Reg is in his room, I think. He needed to catch up on sleep."

"Well, go check. Wake him up," Brune snapped. "I have some things brewing up in the laboratory that may be a more substantial help to our immediate problem," he said.

Lana remembered that Brune had claimed to be something of an alchemist. "Some kind of potions?"

Brune nodded. "After you rouse Partha, go down and see to the main door and the way down to the undercroft, then check those blasted storage doors and see if Raleigh's magic is still holding them together, then find me upstairs," he said. Then he abruptly turned into the round tower and stalked up the stairs.

Tanya came out from the shelter of the kitchen table. She stood, looking around at the mess. The potatoes she'd been peeling were mashed against the walls and scattered on the floor. She sighed and set to work cleaning up the room.

Inga was slower to stand and when she did, she was stiff like a statue, trying her best to vanish into the shadows in the corner. She was whispering something to herself that Lana couldn't make out, but took for some kind of self reassurance.

"I wouldn't worry about dinner, just now," Lana said to the rattled servants and she began up the stairs.

Lana rapped on the door to the room Reg slept in.

"Yes?" the young Partha croaked sleepily.

"Sorry to wake you, but Brune insisted and anyway, it's time. The tower's defenses are beginning to fail," Lana said, peeking her head into the darkened room.

Alert in an instant, Reginald Partha struggled to an upright position. "What should I do?" he asked.

"Go back up to the top of the tower and keep watch. Ring the bell or something if you see anything. I'm going to check the lower levels now." Lana turned back down the stairs that wound through the round tower.

At the bottom was a small round room that contained the iron trapdoor that led to the undercroft.

Where the portals to the elemental realms lie. Where Raleigh is, Lana thought, worrying.

The hatch was secure when Lana pulled on its great ring and she could see the glow of its protective magic with her mage sight.

She stepped into the great hall.

The hearth had a healthy blaze going that appeared, this far, unperturbed, but all of the runes carved into the walls near the ceiling were all ablaze with shifting colored lights that buzzed through the grooves like mad fireflies. The tower was on full alert in every way it could be, and from all directions.

There was a steady and resounding banging on the great metal main door to the tower down the hall and Lana could see mists or steam emanating from all around its seams, but so far, it was still holding.

After watching the steaming door for a minute, Lana made her way up to the store room, and finally to the laboratory way up towards the top of the tower. There, she found Brune leaned over some simmering green liquid in a pot.

He carefully tested the concoction on his tongue after blowing on a spoonful. "Good," he said, satisfied.

On a table, there were laid out several mortars that all contained some mixture of powders. Brune began adding the bubbling liquid from his simmering pot to each in turn as he muttered some kind of incantations to himself.

Lana waited in the doorway until he was finished.

Brune looked at the young blonde Arcana. "Do you know much of alchemy?"

"It's not a field I've much studied," Lana replied.

"No matter. You can still be of assistance," Brune said. "Did you find Partha?"

Lana nodded. "He's gone up to the belfry to keep watch."

"Good." Brune pointed to some empty glass bottles with cork stoppers. "Use this funnel and fill each of those half-way with olive oil." Brune handed Lana a small tin funnel and she set to work as he instructed.

"What will these potions do?" Lana asked as she poured the oil from a round, green flask.

Brune used a pestal to grind and mix the powders in the mortars. "The best anything can do for us. Buy us time, hopefully," he said.

With a clean funnel, he added the powder from the mortars into the bottles Lana had uncorked and poured oil into. Sealing and shaking them to mix all the ingredients, he again intoned some words in the language of magic and Lana was somewhat awed when she saw faint magic auras suddenly appear around the newly enchanted potions. She'd never seen a magic potion created before. It was almost like a new life was created from nothing but dust and sounds.

Brune gathered up the newly created potions into a small sack and tucked it into his belt. "Here. Gather these as well," he said, gesturing to another collection of small glass bottles – potions he'd enchanted earlier. He pushed a small felt bag into Lana's hand.

The lighting in the room changed abruptly when the yellow glow outside ceased and Brune moved closer to one of the windows. Lightning flashed with a great clamor. The hum of the bell was louder from the laboratory and it almost sounded like it tolled with the latest booming thunder. Hail and lightning bolts assailed the tower and water cascaded down the deep-set window panes.

There was a shriek from the stairs. *Inga or Tanya?* Inga, Lana decided. The scream was Inga's.

"Hurry!" Brune said and he dashed down the stairs as Lana finished bagging the remaining potions. Those had a slightly different aura than the ones she'd just witnessed being created.

Well, what are these ones for? I still don't even know what the new ones do, she realized.

With all the remaining potions in her felt bag, Lana raced around the winding stairs, following Brune down to the kitchen, but something caught her attention and she paused on the way down.

A cracked window was leaking rainwater into the round tower's stair and a puddle was forming. She peered closer at the glass pane. It was battered by balls of ice, but some magic was still keeping it from completely shattering.

The cracks are showing and cracks may be all they need, Lana thought.

"You're killing her!" Inga screamed from somewhere below and Lana resumed her dash down the stairs. She could hear Brune repeating some magical phrase as she neared the kitchen.

There, she found Brune gripping Tanya in a tight bear hug as she thrashed in a seemingly uncontrollable spasm in his strong arms. Some kind of vapor was flowing out of her nose and mouth.

"What's… What happened?" Lana was bewildered.

"I am *not* killing her," Brune said through gritted teeth.

Inga didn't seem so sure and had backed away.

Tanya kicked and squirmed, but seemed to be weakening, even as the flow of vapor from her mouth and nose intensified. She shrieked, but it hardly sounded like her own voice. It didn't really sound human for that matter. She went limp in Brune's arms and a cloud of mist that had escaped from Tanya's head flowed up the chimney.

"I think I've discovered the weakest point in the tower's defenses," Brune said grimly. "It's us."

"Us?" Lana repeated.

"Right now, they can't seem to stay long in the tower, but these spirits may be able to possess us. They almost got Tanya, here. A water elemental, I think. It came right out of the kettle, there."

"From the kettle?" Lana was astonished.

"That's where these will come in useful," Brune said, reaching one hand towards the felt bag Lana held. She handed it over to him. In Brune's other arm, Tanya was mostly limp and semiconscious, but he managed to fish a potion bottle out and uncork it one-handed while continuing to support Tanya with his other arm. She seemed to be slowly coming back to her senses.

Lana was astonished to see Brune bring the open bottle to Tanya's lips.

"What are you doing?" Lana shouted in fear and shock.

"This potion will offer some resistance to the elementals' magic," Brune explained, holding the potion forward.

"*No*, Brune! Are you mad, giving magic to peasants? You can't do that! It's forbidden!"

"We need every possible advantage," Brune said. "This will make them stronger and better able to resist."

Lana shook her head emphatically. "You can't do this. You'll bring the dark stalkers down on us. You'll bring the whole damn Empire down on us. You mustn't!"

"I must and I will! Besides, the dark stalkers are a myth. Or, at least, their power to sniff out magical aberrations is a myth. No one will ever need to know."

"Noooo!!!" Lana rushed forward, but Brune spoke a few harsh syllables with a finger extended in her direction and she froze in her tracks, paralyzed by Brune's spell, just as Gavin had been helplessly caught in it.

Brune tipped the potion to Tanya's lips. "Drink this," he said, calmly. "It will protect you."

Tanya drank down the potion as Lana watched helplessly.

The bell tolled.

The Wind Makers

After narrowly escaping becoming a pet of Geshalla's over an unlikely pact involving peaches, Raleigh further inured himself to the three slyphs as they came to understand his fight was with a common enemy.

Raleigh learned Geshalla, Wawasha and Swish each harbored a particularly vehement hatred of the elemental prince called Grashnuk. They were almost giddy to help point Raleigh in the right direction – if there was such a thing as direction in this realm – to advance his fight against the rebellious wind spirit.

Space and travel seemed somewhat abstract and ineffable in the elemental realm. Raleigh felt strongly that he was in a dream-state, even though he was certain everything he was experiencing was both conscious and consequential.

Movement was especially surreal in the sky realm. *Did I move or did a new environment just form around me?* Raleigh thought as he learned to go from one fixed point to another by sheer force of will.

There was also an attractive force, just as the earth in his own realm pulled him down. Patches of land that floated here and there in the endless sky became "down" if he focused on them, so he could "fall" in any direction – up, down or sideways towards any tangible features he happened to come across. Even the occasional cloud formation could exert a gravitational pull if he let it.

With help from the slyphs, he was learning to control his movement and they finally guided him to the Palace of the Winds, where he hoped to secure an audience with Ouranos, the king of this strange sky realm and find a way to defeat that king's own estranged son.

The palace, as it was called, looked more like a village that was scattered across a series of islands in the sky, arranged in concentric circles and at different altitudes from one another. The "rooms" of the palace were mostly open-air spaces demarcated by pillars and archways of stone and water, or simply by the arrangement of furnishings in the space.

Like gardens in the sky, some looked rather like flying gazebos to Raleigh.

It wasn't difficult to pick out King Ouranos holding court on a large central disc. Wispy, insubstantial things swirled around the king, like gauze and smoke and he was cloaked in wind and shadows that glinted with sparkling frost.

The king of the winds was a giant figure, crackling with power and fury, but at the same time his very existence seemed fleeting, as if he swelled and faded like the winds he commanded.

Raleigh guessed Ouranos must be twenty-feet tall and half as broad.

The king was surrounded by elemental spirits – most of the wind, but some from other realms. A few water elementals and rocky creatures of the earth also attended court. Slyphs flitted about here and there, too.

The sound of a hundred breezes rose and fell, mingled with the gurgling murmur of water flowing in fountains and graceful arcs.

The huge floating disk that served as the throne room in the Palace of the Winds was elaborately adorned with green topiaries, ponds and a hundred pennants of myriad colors that snapped easily in the light winds that flowed around it.

The slyphs had directed Raleigh to a smaller island in the orbit of the king's court. It wasn't much more than a floating rock with a roughly level surface. There were a couple tall stone arches at the edges.

Raleigh guessed it to be some kind of antechamber where outsiders might wait to petition the king. He stood on the small island, alone and afraid. He had no idea how these alien and tremendously powerful elemental creatures would take his presence in their realm.

Raleigh marveled at the open air palace suspended in the vast blue expanse and all of its denizens, but it wasn't long before the king himself took notice of the nervous human.

"Mageborn Talanth!" The king's voice was a gale. "You are welcome in my palace. Why have you ventured to my realm?"

Raleigh hadn't moved, but suddenly, he was before the giant king on the central island. "Whoa," he said involuntarily, taking a stumbling step backward.

The king's yellow-green eyes pierced through his shadowy visage and regarded Raleigh intently.

The young Talanth could feel a touch of the power of the king from his gaze alone.

"Mighty King Ouranos," Raliegh began, not entirely sure of the right protocol or mode of address for the situation, "I beseech you for an audience, for I come with a grievance."

"You already have your audience, Talanth-child," The king's windy voice noted.

Raleigh nodded, swallowed and pressed on. "I have come from the Painted Tower, which, at this very moment is besieged by elemental spirits."

Raleigh felt like the king's gaze was piercing right into his soul, but the king of the winds said nothing.

"Ancient pacts between our peoples ratified the sovereignty of the borderlands between our realms, yet some of your kind seek to breach them. The tower that guards the borders is under attack. My world itself is under threat of invasion by beings who should be subjects of your rule."

The king tilted his shadowed head, but still didn't reply.

One of them spoke to me," Raleigh forged ahead. "He said he was called Grashnuk…"

The king answered that. "Grashnuk? Grashnuk, you say?" The king's voice was a hurricane. "My wayward son spoke to you?"

"Yes, your… majesty?"

"What did the prince want with you, Talanth-child?" Ouranos' voice trailed off with a rumble like distant, rolling thunder.

"Well, in essence, he, uh, just wanted me to die," Raleigh said. "He demanded that my fellows and I abandon the tower to him, if we wanted swift and painless deaths. We've held out this long, but three magi are dead in the tower and still others were killed or lost when a tempest of supernatural power appeared in the vicinity. The Painted Tower seems well-defended by old magic, but it isn't invincible and it will eventually fall, I'm sure. Probably very soon."

"If Grashnuk takes your tower, he and his allies will be free to fully emerge in your realm," The king thundered. "The power they have in your world now is nothing compared to what it will be. Grashnuk respects nothing. He abides no law. That is why I banished him from my court and that is why he seeks entry into your world – to establish a kingdom of his own, away from my realm."

The situation was dire, but hearing Ouranos explain in those terms shook Raliegh to his core.

"In my kingdom, we still honor the old pacts we made with mortals, even if many of your kind have forgotten them," Ouranos boomed. "I will lend aid to keep sacrosanct our borders and our ancient treaties."

"I thank you, Mighty King Ouranos."

"There is a solution to your dilemma, I think and it could perhaps solve one of mine as well." The king's voice breezed and then gusted. "Ranius, your ancestor who built the tower you and your friends now defend never completely finished his design. He had wrought a mighty artifact – one that frightened me. It was to be the pinnacle of the structure's power, but I made a bargain with him and obtained that artifact to keep it from integrating with the tower."

Raleigh was rapt. *Ranius! I knew it!*

"I'll return it to you if you will swear to use it to defeat Grashnuk and defend your tower and work no additional mischief with it." For a twenty-foot giant with command of the air itself, Ouranos sounded a little uncertain.

"What is it?" Raleigh was enraptured by fascination.

"It's a lightning rod, or so it was named by the mage who made it," Ouranos replied. "Its a metal rod that can contain and command one of our kind. And unlike other lightning rods of your mortal realm, it doesn't attract lightning. It will summon it. I couldn't countenance such a powerful weapon against my own kind in the hands of the mageborn, so we made a pact and traded some of our magics to the magi in exchange for the rod being given over to my keeping."

"Your majesty, if you entrust me with my ancestor's artifact, I swear to use it only to defeat Grashnuk and defend the tower."

The giant king of the winds sighed. "I honor the old pacts. I will help you preserve the boundaries between the realms. I will give you the rod. Then it will be up to you. Do you agree?"

The Tower, Cracked

The great bell had been humming for days, just from vibrations from the otherworldly storm penetrating the tower's structure, but to hear it ring was stunning. Its tone was pure and resounding. Lana knew it meant Reg had spotted some new imminent danger from his perch in the belfry.

There was power in the tolling of the bell, Lana perceived. She felt something, but she didn't have the faintest idea what it might mean for their predicament. Maybe nothing. It felt like there was supposed to be something more, kind of like when one of her spells failed.

After Brune had administered his potions to both of the servant girls, he released Lana from his magical grip and offered a bottle back to her.

"One in, all in, I suppose," Lana said, accepting the bottle and pulling out its cork stopper. Giving magic to non-magi was among the Empire's highest crimes, but there was no undoing what Brune had done.

There may come consequences, though.

The dark stalkers were creatures that lived somewhere on the borderlands between myths and secrets. They were said to be human-like creatures without normal eyesight, but able to sniff out aberrations of magic with their notedly prominent noses, not to mention their purported demonic powers.

Lana, like all young magi, had been taught that those who broke the highest laws of magic, be they commoner or mage would be hunted down by the stalkers.

Lana's outlook was grim, though she'd survived this far. *Still, I'd hate to survive this only to have the dark stalkers come and rend my soul after.*

Lana hoped that Brune was right, that their existence or abilities were exaggerated and she stuffed those fears aside. There were more immediate threats for the nonce.

Lana swallowed the bitter concoction Brune had mixed up and could immediately feel the warm touch of magic spread throughout her body. It was a comforting sensation. "Right," she said. "I'll go see what Reg has spotted," and she started up the stairs.

Around the bend a story up, Lana was confronted on the stairs by a seven-foot tall, man-shaped creature, who appeared to be formed entirely of water.

Lana hesitated, but the creature did not. It swung a huge, watery fist, overhand, so that it crashed down on Lana's head.

The elemental fist didn't make a solid connection, consisting only of liquid, but the sheer volume and force of the water slamming into her knocked her to her knees and into the outer wall. She was stunned and utterly soaked through, from her blonde hair to her black stockings. It felt like she'd belly flopped into a river from a hundred-foot cliff.

You're the window leak, she thought dazedly, before she tried to get back to her feet.

The water elemental moved in, with both its arms outstretched.

Lana instinctively cast the first spell that came to mind. "Fajrojetos!" she exclaimed, pointing at the creature with her right hand. Flames burst forth from her finger in a powerful jet, creating considerable steam when it impacted the huge elemental, but accomplishing little else.

The creature lunged forward, engulfing Lana with its huge watery arms and then with its entire body. Lana was inside the elemental!

Panic was rising as Lana realized she couldn't breathe and she tried to fight her way out of the creature's liquid form. Whichever way she moved, it matched her direction and the living water buffeted her back as well, like dashing into the surf.

Lana heard a muffled voice call out in the language of magic, "Vaporigi!" and in a sudden eruption of hot steam, she was free. The water elemental vanished, leaving only puddles on the stairs where its imposing form had trod.

She turned around to see where the voice had come from. "Raleigh!"

The young Talanth had saved her for a second time, so by her reckoning, they were even.

Raleigh seemed in good health and was resplendent in his maroon robes. He carried what looked like an iron staff with a loop for a finial. It came to a point at its base. Lana had never seen Raleigh with a staff of any kind before.

From above them, the bell tolled again.

"What's that about?" Raleigh asked.

"Reg is on lookout up in the belfry. I'd guess he's signaling yet another new threat," Lana said, sitting down on the step. She needed to catch her breath. "Am I ever glad to see you!"

"Likewise," Raleigh replied, glancing beyond Lana and up the stairs.

"Yes. I was just on my way up there, but I got a little distracted," Lana said apologetically. "Give me a second. Did you find what you were after?" Lana got back to her feet.

Raleigh hefted the iron staff. "I hope so."

"So do I. Alright. Let's go see." Lana led the way up to the belfry.

Reg was looking out the rain-streaked windows into the dark and stormy chaos swirling all around the tower, a mostly useless spyglass in his hand.

"Raleigh!" the young Partha enthused.

"What have you seen, Reg?" Raleigh asked.

"Well, unless I'm mistaken, I've seen our aspiring torturer and murderer, himself," Reg said.

"Indeed? Grashunk? Where?" Raleigh's curiosity was piqued.

"He's right out in front of the door," Reg said, pointing.

"May I?" Raleigh leaned his iron staff against a window and reached a hand towards the spyglass.

"Of course." Reg handed it over.

"My," Raleigh commented, looking through the lens, down at the front of the tower. "He is a sight, isn't he? Yes. I'm sure that's Grashnuk. Looks a bit like his father, only meaner and nastier."

"His father??" Reg and Lana reacted as one.

Raleigh handed the spyglass to Lana so she could see the villain responsible for all the misery and misfortune that had befallen them.

Grashnuk was shrouded in mists and shadows and appeared only semi-substantial, but his transparent shape was of a giant man who glowed with tremendous magic power. If he had a face, it was hidden behind an armored mask that resembled an elongated human skull. Green eyes glowed brightly behind the metal facade.

Dozens of mudmen and water spirits surrounded the elemental prince and multi-colored lightning flashed all around.

"Yes. I had an audience with Ouranos, king of the winds." Raleigh related. It was he who gave me this." Raleigh pointed to the staff. "He said it was a 'lightning rod,' but I don't think that does it justice."

"I don't see how a lightning rod is any use, now. The tower's probably been struck a hundred times, just while you were away," Reg said.

"That's not all it's for." Raleigh replied. "This was originally meant to be a part of this tower's defenses, but Ranius bartered it away to King Ouranos instead of finishing it. I'm going to install it and complete the tower."

Lana set the spyglass on a window ledge. "What will that do?" she asked with a hint of skepticism.

"Hopefully, it will put an end to our Grashnuk problem for good," Raleigh replied. "But, we'll have to open the door and let him in, first."

A Plan

Raleigh had gathered everyone in the great hall on the tower's main floor to tell his tale of meeting King Ouranos in the sky realm and to explain his plan.

Some kind of thick vapor was emanating copiously from the seam around the great metal door, but thus far, it hadn't manifested into another invader. The runes around the ceiling line were aglow with a dizzying array of multi-colored lights zipping to and fro to urgently alert the occupants of the tower to what they already knew. They were surrounded on all sides and even from another dimension, while Grashnuk demanded to be heeded.

Raleigh held forth the iron staff with a loop at its apex. "According to the king of the winds, this metal rod was created by Ranius himself to be a part of this tower's defenses. With it, I hope to capture Grashnuk and further use it's power to banish the other elemental spirits besieging us under his command."

"How will you do that?" Brune asked simply.

"There is a room near the top of the round tower that will help facilitate the binding."

"That door that's always locked?" Lana asked excitedly. "I wondered what could be in there!"

"I've learned that it's a summoning chamber and it will open for me, now. It's also useful for binding spirits," Raleigh said.

"Then, I'll have to climb up to the top of the belfry turret to install the rod and that will complete the tower's magic."

"With Grashnuk trapped in it?" Lana put in.

"Well, yes. He will become part of the tower's enchantment, actually," Raleigh replied.

"Forever?" Inga surprised everyone by speaking up.

The conversation was mage business, but Raliegh humored the commoner's curiosity. Others might wonder about Grashnuk's fate, anyway. "Yes. Forever."

"Pressed into eternal service for one's enemy... I almost pity him... it if works," Lana said.

"Yes. As long as nothing goes wrong. He'll mostly sleep, though," Raleigh said. "I had a teacher who explained this to me. There's a consciousness of a sort in all magic items but only when animated. When magic sleeps, it dreams. So, Grashnuk will dream, and he will only awaken when the rod is invoked in defense of the tower."

"How fitting," Brune said. "But how do you intend to get Grashnuk into this special room where you will capture him in the first place?"

That's when Raleigh got nervous. He licked his lips and said, "We'll simply open the door and let him in."

Brune's bright blue eyes locked onto Raleigh's hazel eyes and held his gaze steady. "Raleigh. Besides Grashnuk, we are surrounded by a menagerie of elemental spirits. We can't risk letting them all in at once. One alone is trying enough to deal with. There must be dozens..."

"Hundreds, actually," Raleigh said. "I could see their shadows all around the tower when I made my way back through the portal. Grashnuk has moved his whole camp right on top of us."

"You've gone mad," Brune said. "Or else you're possessed by one of Grashnuk's servants."

"What other choice do we have?" asked Lana. "If he's right, we can end this siege and get away with our lives. It can be over tonight." she pointed out.

"If he's wrong he's killed us all and not to mention that this elemental rebellion could have profound consequences for the region. The tower has to hold," said Brune.

"If we just keep trying to defend the tower as the windows crack and the walls crumble around us, we're eventually going to lose. Grashnuk will kill us. Actually, he'll torture us for a couple decades, first and *then* he'll kill us," Reg said.

"What do we do?" Brune asked with an air of exasperated resignation.

"The belfry is the most defensible spot in the tower," Raleigh said. "There is only one door in or out. I propose all of you gather in there. I will wait for Grashnuk in the conjuration room."

"What about the undercroft?" Brune suggested. "If things don't go as you hope, perhaps there's a chance we could use the portal to escape into another realm."

"Better than certain death by torture," Reg added.

Raleigh shook his head. "Grashnuk's army have taken control of the portal from the other side. I nearly didn't make it back, but for help from some slyphs who took a liking to me. It's impossible, now."

"Can they use the portal to enter the tower?" Lana asked.

"No. I... Well, I don't think so. There are wards to prevent that." Raleigh was less than sure. "At any rate we haven't much time. One way or another, Grashnuk and his minions are going to get in to this tower. So, let's get on with it," he said with an air of finality.

"How can we be certain Grashnuk will go to you in the summoning room? He might just as well go into the Whisper Room and wouldn't he work mischief in there?" Reg inquired.

"I admit, that could be bad," Raleigh said. The tower obeys my will, though and that door will be sealed.

"I created some expanding force wall potions that we could use to help guide Grashnuk up to you," Brune said. "They only last a few minutes at best, but they're strong enough to stop just about anything."

"That could help," Raleigh said, looking around the room. His gaze passed over Inga and Tanya, but then snapped back to the two commoners. "Why am I detecting a magic aura from your servants, Lord DeVon?"

"I gave them each a potion to ward off magical assault on their minds. They were a dangerous liability, otherwise," Brune said. "I have one for you as well."

Raleigh just frowned in thought for a moment, then nodded. "Fine. Good. Maybe they can help, too, then. Give everyone one of your force wall potions and we'll use them to corral and guide Grashnuk as necessary to make sure he finds his way to the summoning room and at the same time, hold his minions at bay — hopefully long enough for me to finish the task."

Brune distributed his potions and provided necessary instructions for their use. It was simple enough. One just poured it in a line on the ground and an invisible wall of magic force would spring into being and stretch to fill whatever space was available.

Brune handed Raleigh a small bottle of the potion that was supposed to protect against magical attack. Raleigh regarded the small vial with suspicion for a moment.

Brune's eyes narrowed. "If you die, surely I'll be right behind you," he said.

Raleigh shrugged and swallowed the potion and they finalized the details of the risky plan.

Everyone had one force wall in their pocket and they were stationed strategically throughout the tower, while Raleigh and Reginald ascended the stairs, first to the Whisper Room.

First, to pique his pride, Raleigh thought.

The door to the Whisper Room swung open as Raleigh alit on its landing. He walked into the small semi-circular room in the round tower and planted his feet on the rectangular metal plates that were set in the wooden floor.

He felt a jolt as energy flowed up one leg and down the other and then he heard Grashnuk's terrible, screaming whispers.

"Have you come to your senses, mage?" the rogue elemental prince seethed through the ether.

"Mighty Grashnuk, we know we are beaten," Raleigh said into the big sideways basin on the wall. "Your power is too vast for us to withstand any longer."

That much was true.

"I beg you, oh, great, wise and powerful prince of the winds, please spare my companions from your wroth and I will surrender myself to your just judgment. Attempting to resist your might was entirely my doing. Do not hold it against them. I alone am responsible."

"You are a foolish mortal," Grashnuk said. "I will destroy you, but I may find the generosity to temper my rage and kill your friends more quickly."

"I thank you, mighty Grashnuk. I will open the door to you and await your judgment."

Raleigh stepped off the brass plates. "I'm done," he said to Reg. "Go down to Davis' room and lock the door tight. Use the force wall potion if Grashnuk of any of his minions attempt to enter. Be ready to seal the tower back up once Grashnuk is inside."

The red-robed young mage nodded. "Good luck, Raleigh," he said.

Raleigh went across the landing into the storage room and picked up two sacks of flour, then made his way up to the summoning chamber and the door opened for him.

Nervous energy was crawling from his stomach to his extremities as he studied the room. Red arcane markings were painted all over the floor. In the middle was a large eight-pointed star in a circle.

Raleigh set the flour sacks down and then tore them open to scatter the tan powder all over the floor, hiding its markings.

Next, he leaned the iron staff on a small pedestal that was plated with brass. He threw the empty burlap sacks over that.

Finally, after quickly running through his mind what he'd been told by Ouranos and what he'd read in the library, he took a deep breath, then willed the tower to open the main door.

I hope everyone is ready down there, he thought. *I hope I'm ready.*

He stood opposite the door and waited.

Reg

Davis Talanth's bedroom was a very small cell accessed on the ground floor from the great hall. The two outside walls of the space were of the multi-hued stone the tower was named for and the other two were knotty pine. On the long pine wall, there were a couple shelves and drawers built-in. Two small landscape paintings also decorated it, but another of that wall's features was the reason Reg had stationed himself in Davis' old room.

Behind one of the paintings was a peephole that looked out into the entryway, where the cloaks were hung. It was essentially undetectable from the other side, but afforded a wide-angled view of the short wooden passage from the main door to the great hall.

Reg took in the room. He was in there from time to time to change the bedclothes as part of his upkeep duties as Vardan's apprentice and he knew old Davis hadn't kept many personal possessions. His books, he'd added to the tower's collection when he moved in. He didn't seem to own any magical devices that Reg knew of.

It was a slippery thought, that Davis was dead, along with Reginald's master, Vardan. When Reg considered it, he was surprised and saddened anew as if just hearing the news.

That still hasn't sunk in. There's been no time for anything to really sink in.

Reg pulled open one of the drawers and found a considerable stash of gold and gems stowed inside. It was to be expected that Davis, lord of the Painted Tower would have accumulated some money over his lifetime, but Reg was stunned to suddenly see it. It was sad and sobering to realize that all that remained of the man was some unspent material wealth.

Fat lot of good it'll do you, now.

He closed the drawer.

With death literally at the door, Reg considered what he might leave behind. *Outside my parents, the world will never know I even existed if I die with these strangers.* Any moment now and Raleigh would be opening that front door to admit their proclaimed death, Grashnuk into the tower.

Raleigh wouldn't be able to see him enter, tucked away on an upper level of the round tower as he was. So, Reg was responsible for closing the door once the errant prince of the winds was within.

He heard it. The big metal door began its creaking and scraping arc, exposing the entry to the fury of the intensifying storm raging outside. Wind blasted rain and hail into the entry as Reg peered on it through the peephole.

It was less than a minute before the silver mask and glowing green eyes of Grashnuk appeared at the threshold. His body was a foggy whirl of rain and ice in the wind. His cloak, shadows.

The wind elemental looked left and right, then down the hall before proceeding, but seeing nothing, he blew down the short corridor with a woosh and disappeared from Reginald's view.

Reg turned his attention back to the main door and willed it to close, even as he saw the mudman appear in the entry.

Oh, crumbs!

Reg silently urged the door to close faster, but it was too late. The earth elemental was also in the tower, now.

The door finished closing with a thud.
The mudman sloshed down the corridor to the great hall.

Raleigh

Raleigh didn't have to wait long. Just a minute after he'd willed the tower door to open, Grashnuk appeared in the doorway to the small round room.

The rogue prince of the winds appeared as a dark shape, cloaked in frost and shadow, the light of his blazing green eyes piercing his silver skull mask. Raleigh felt a cold breeze from the wind prince's mere presence. It stirred up dust and the flour he'd scattered all over the floor.

Oh, no! The flour! Raleigh thought. *I hadn't considered that!*

"There you are!" Grashnuk exuded. "I could smell your blood from the moment I entered."

"The tower is yours," Raleigh said, sinking down onto his knees. He looked downward in defeat and averting his gaze from Grashnuk's majesty.

"*You're* mine now as well, mageborn worm!" Grashnuk's fury filled the room. His translucent form seemed to darken.

It was a frightful display but Raleigh was mostly concerned about the flour blowing away as the elemental's own wind swelled with his shrill and shouting voice. He was increasingly worried that the summoning and binding markings on the floor would be revealed too soon.

"I submit to your wise judgment, mighty Grashnuk," Raleigh said meekly.

Just come in. Come get me, you blustering windbag!

Grashnuk himself grew. He literally seemed to swell with pride. The wind intensified. The flour swirled around.

Raleigh winced as the magic symbols were becoming fleetingly visible beneath a virtual dustdevil.

Then Grashnuk, full of his own triumph, stepped into the room without any notice of the floor.

Raleigh sprang to his feet.

"Estu nemovebla, eksterulo!" he shouted.

"What? What is this?" Grashnuk screamed.

"Estu nemovebla, eksterulo!" Raleigh chanted. The eight-pointed star that Grashnuk now stood in the center of began to emit a light through the swirls of tan powder and duplicates of the symbol rose up, like several individual layers of paint had peeled up from the floor, except they were comprised only of red light. The floating stars began rotate in rows around Grashnuk.

Lana appeared behind Grashnuk on the stairs, holding a vial of the forcewall potion Brune had provided.

Raleigh shook his head to let Lana know the potion wasn't needed. Grashnuk was already trapped by the magic planted there by Raleigh's ancestor.

The elemental prince roared in anger and alarm. He tried to retreat back out of the room, but found himself imprisoned within the octagonal inner lines of the glowing stars.

Grashnuk glared at Raleigh for a second, but then suddenly laughed. Gales of the elemental prince's booming mirth filled the small binding chamber.

"You arrogant fool. You can't imprison me!" guffawed the elemental prince.

Inga

"I feel so warm and tingly," Tanya whispered.

"I know! I feel it, too," Inga whispered back excitedly. She felt warm and she felt strong. Magic energy pulsed through her body, creating a sensation she couldn't have even imagined before. Brune's protective potion made her feel safe. More than that, almost invincible.

It also felt like she was wrapped in the softest, warm blankets and she was as light as air. A faint, but pleasant tingling sensation buzzed though her being.

I wouldn't even have the words to try to describe this, Inga thought. But, Tanya was experiencing it with her.

The servant girls exchanged a meaningful look they each understood.

They had been charged, with their master, to prevent Grashnuk entering the Whisper Room. Lord Raleigh had sealed it with the tower's magic, but just to be sure, Lord Brune DeVon along with his servants, Inga and Tanya, were all ready with force wall potions.

They had gathered in the kitchen as a staging point. Lord Brune was listening at the stairwell outside the door. "Hush!" He hissed. "Alright, now, Inga, hurry up to the storage room," he said, coming back into the room. "When you hear me whistle, use the potion on the stairway. Got it?"

"Yes, m'lord."

"Good. Hurry. Go."

With pulse-pounding enthusiasm, Inga dashed up the stone steps to the landing that was shared by the Whisper Room in the round tower and the square tower's adjacent third-floor storage room. She stepped into the dark space, where she'd seen Lord Reginald fly out the big wooden doors that even now seemed strained to keep the storm out as they banged and rattled against forces of nature and magic.

She was thrilled. Once, she could scarcely dream about glimpsing for herself, the opulence of the mage lords' lives, but now, she knew what it felt like to be one of them.

Or I'm guessing it's something at least kind-of like this, she thought. It felt good! *I never want this feeling to end.*

Breathing deeply, Inga gripped the force wall potion her master gave her in her right hand.

It seemed like mere moments before she heard her signal. Lord Brune's lilting whistle resounded up the circular stair and Inga was ready to act.

With a glance at the vial in her hand, she stepped out onto the landing to come, unexpectedly, face to face with the mudman.

The huge, dripping, lumbering, roughly-man-shaped giant of a creature didn't frighten Inga, even as it raised it's massive arm.

Its fist was a twenty-pound ball of mud, though and it knocked Inga off her feet and up a few stairs. She slammed hard into the wall and stone steps, but was amazed to find herself uninjured. She was a little stunned, but got straight to her feet.

The mudman advanced, raising it's huge, slimy, brown-gray fist again.

Inga pulled the cork and upended her potion bottle, pouring its contents out in a line across the stairway.

The mudman struck. His sludgy fist splattered apart like a mudpie hitting a window pane when it hit the invisible barrier Inga had just conjured.

Protected by magic within, now she *wielded* magic without. Inga stopped an actual monster with it and for the first time in her life, she felt *powerful*.

Tanya and Brune appeared behind the dripping, raging beast, having come up from the kitchen.

Tanya stood back, potion vial in hand, ready.

Brune raised his hands towards the mudman's back. He intoned a series of harsh magical words, concluding, "Mortigi forton" and the stairway darkened. An unnatural, cold energy vibrated the air.

The mudman, engulfed by Brune's deadly magic, appeared to writhe in pain as it's dripping, slimy form rapidly disintegrated, collapsing into it's base constituent until it was no more than an inanimate pile of sopping mud, oozing slowly down the cold, red, stone steps.

"Whoo!" Inga shouted with a hop.

The Wrath of Ranius

Trapped by magic set up in the tower centuries ago by Raleigh's ancestor Ranius, Grashnuk did not seem in the least concerned. In fact, he laughed as the red glowing eight pointed stars twisted slowly around his ghostly body.

"Your mortal magic can't stop me, mage," said the exiled prince of winds. His voice sounded like rustling leaves, but it filled the small room with menace.

Raleigh pulled the burlap sacks off the big Iron staff he had resting against the bronze-plated pedestal and Grashnuk seemed to recognize the object.

"Where? Where did you get that?" Now, the elemental prince didn't seem as sure of himself. "No!" Grashnuk thrashed against the red octagonal lines around him, but he could not immediately break free of the magical cage.

"You don't belong here, Grashnuk. You've contravened ancient pacts between our people and your father has helped me to put things right!" Raleigh said, thrusting the looped end of the staff forward, towards Grashnuk.

He put his other hand on the pedestal and began to chant. "Farigu unu kun la kunlaborantaro! Vi estas ligita, por ciam! Farigu unu kun la kunlaborantaro! Vi estas ligita, por ciam!"

"My father?! I'll destroy him too! I'll destroy you all!" Grashnuk's rage was a whirlwind – for a moment. Then, he was

161

shrinking as his essence was drawn into the iron staff. Frost and shadows and sparkling energy flowed from the eight-pointed stars to the staff as Grashnuk became one with the black iron.

"Farigu unu kun la kunlaborantaro! Vi estas ligita, por ciam!"

Grashnuk's fading last words were "Raleigh Talanth, I will revisit vengeance upon you and all your family!"

Then he was gone and the room fell still as the glowing red magic faded.

Grashnuk was bound to the iron staff – the great lightning rod created long ago by Ranius to be the very pinnacle of the Painted Tower. Now Raleigh had to get it up there before Grashnuk's multitude of elemental allies further breached the weakened tower's defenses.

"Lana!" Raleigh called out.

She was still waiting outside the summoning and binding room. "I'm here!" she peeked her blonde head around the door jamb.

"Lana, we have to get this up to the peak of the belfry," Raleigh said, hefting the iron staff. He could feel power and fury thrumming through it, now. It was abuzz in his hands. He could see it's bright magic aura in the dim, circular room.

She nodded.

"We have to be quick. I'll need you to open the belfry windows and hold off any intruders long enough for me to get this in place. Then, ring the bell. Do you follow me?"

"I understand, Raleigh. I'm ready. Let's go!"

The two sprinted up the winding stairs to the highest room in the structure – the belfry atop the round tower.

Lana found the crank that would open all the belfry's thick glass windows at once.

"Wait until I give the word," Raleigh said. He went out into the observation room atop the square tower and, with a deep breath opened a door out onto the misty parapet.

The walkway around the high top of the tall square tower was under assault by the elements. Wind whipped the rain and hail around so hard it felt like bullets from a hundred slings launched at him at once as he stepped out into the freezing air.

The lightning was constant and blinding. The thunder rolled on as a deafening continuous rumbling – like an earthquake combined with a volcanic eruption.

Raleigh knew he'd have to work fast before the elemental spirits besieging the tower noticed him up on the battlements or found opportunity in the soon-to-be open belfry windows.

He crouched low, trying to keep below the merlons that surrounded the parapet, both to be less noticeable and to reduce his exposure to the punishing elements.

The walkway was flooded with black, icy water, but near crawling, Raleigh made his way slowly to the turret housing the tower's great bell.

With the strap from one of his bags and the belt from his robe, he tied the heavy, vibrating iron staff to his back, then reached up to grasp a cold wet stone that jutted slightly out from the round tower.

The stonework was deliberately uneven here to create a sort-of crude ladder, but it was never meant to be used in inclement weather, let alone a supernatural storm.

The stones were slippery. The wind was blustery. Hail pummeled the young Talanth as he got his second foot off the parapet and into a nook in the stone wall. His fingers were already feeling stiff from the cold as he reached for the next handhold.

Slowly, Raleigh ascended. One treacherous foothold, one slick handhold at a time as icy, wet wind lashed his face, and yanked at his robes.

His right foot slipped out, causing his face to collide with the cold rough stone, but he held himself in place with the diminishing strength of his hands.

He reached the mossy shingles of the conical roof, which would have been an impossible surface to climb further up, but there were iron grips shaped about like horse shoes set every few feet to allow climbing for maintenance.

Arms numb and shaking, he hauled himself slowly up onto the slimy moss and lichen-covered roof, where there was no shelter at all from the rain, ice and wind.

Raleigh looked down and saw that Lana had positioned herself halfway out the door onto the parapet so she could watch his assent.

He was about twenty feet above the stone parapet and well over a hundred feet from the dark ground, below.

Pulling together all the determination he had left, he climbed the last few iron rungs, standing, balanced precariously on the final one. It was only wide enough for one foot.

At the apex of the conical roof, there was a series of steel rings fastened to three rods that protruded from the rooftop. In the middle of those, Raleigh could see a hole right at the roof's point.

With one hand gripping the iron contraption at the peak, he used the other – carefully – to loosen the staff strapped to his back, and finally, balancing on one foot in the winds and rain at the top of the Painted Tower, he inserted Ranius' lightning rod where it was always meant to be.

He waved down at Lana "Now!" Raleigh shouted. "Open the windows and ring the bell! Hurry!"

On the dark parapet below, Lana nodded under her black hood and disappeared back into the tower.

Hand over hand, Raleigh slowly lowered himself back down the roof. When he was halfway down, the bell tolled.

The resounding tone was pure and deep and it momentarily drowned out all the din of the storm. Raleigh felt the sound penetrate through every iota of his being.

Then, a dazzling conjunction of lightning met at the iron staff Raleigh had just installed. Dozens and dozens of brilliant, zig-zagging bolts streaking from all directions of the stormy sky struck Ranius' lightning rod.

Just as quickly, lightning bolts began striking the ground all around the tower, but this time they were coming from the rod itself! The lightning rod was *emitting* lightning.

Raleigh had to close his eyes against the repeated, brilliant flashes of energy as he fell the rest of the way back down to the flooded stone parapet.

Power flowed, streaking and forking, scorching through the air and targeting anything the tower didn't find welcome. The blinding spectacle continued for several minutes until Grashnuk's elemental army, spirits of the skies, the earth and the sea were all gone. They were utterly destroyed, or banished back to their home realms. Raleigh wasn't sure of which, but when the lightning finally stopped, the siege was over and Grashnuk slept.

Epilogue

Inga thought often about her time in the painted tower. Returning to Devonshire and adjusting to the mundane life of a common servant had proven unexpectedly difficult and, though she was ever diligent about her duties, it chafed her, sometimes.

She set a dish on a large serving tray, nudging and shuffling the others already on it to make everything fit nicely and neatly.

Her mind wandered as she worked. Her hands knew the job.

During the ordeal at the tower, all she wished for was to make it back to her home at Devonshire alive. Now she found that she wanted more. More than survival. More than existence. Her experience with magic had teased her with infinite possibilities.

So, she toiled and obeyed as her master Brune expected, but she also took every opportunity to learn whatever she could – about anything and everything.

She fetched a kettle and filled a cup with mulled mead, then fit it in to her arrangement.

It sounded impossible, even to herself, but Inga determined that she would not be a simple servant for the rest of her life. Somehow, some way, she would take control of her own destiny and she would taste *power* again.

She didn't share any of those thoughts with anyone, of course. Not even Tanya. Despite sharing nearly identical experiences,

Tanya seemed unchanged by the whole adventure. She was quite content to carry on serving the DeVons, just as she always had.

Tanya had been jubilant the day they departed from the Painted Tower. Getting back to the ordinary drudgery of servitude was apparently all she could conceive as "good."

Once Lord Raleigh had full control of the tower, between himself, Lord Brune and the young Lord Partha, they'd worked out how to use the Whisper Room everyone seemed to be arguing about before and they got word to Devonshire.

As the sun shone again and the muddy lands dried, Lord Alaric DeVon sent carriages to retrieve them all, including Lord Gavin's corpse.

While Tanya had been practically dancing on air to be on the road to home, Inga felt sadness and a longing.

The other magi were preparing to go off in other directions, on new adventures of their own. Inga almost wished she could have joined them. Raleigh had seemed very kind, for a mage.

Inga had been surprised that the young Talanth lord didn't stay to lay claim to the tower once he had full control of it. The lady Arcana had suggested that he probably could, but he didn't seem interested. He'd said something about going west to some dreadful sounding place called the Desert of the Dead. He'd also become strangely obsessed with where he could find some peaches.

None of that could begin until after he'd seen to it that some other members of his clan with proper ranks and titles arrived to take over the stewardship of the Painted Tower, of course.

While they had been waiting for the carriages to arrive from Devonshire, one more unexpected visitor happened upon the tower. He was a gaunt, near-starved young mage about the same age as Lady Arcana and it turned out that they were acquainted.

Lord Arvin Happ, he was called and Inga had been enchanted by the beautiful purple hue of his rather tattered robes.

Lady Arcana had cried when she greeted the young Happ, Inga recalled.

Apparently, he'd been hiding out in a small cave not far away, to weather the storm.

Since Lord Reginald Partha's master, Lord Vardan Talanth had been killed by Grashnuk, there had been no reason for him to stay at the tower, either, and so he joined up with Lady Arcana and her purple-robed friend to go off to who-knows-where.

Inga thought frequently of those other magi and the frightful days and nights they'd all spent together in the Painted Tower. She thought of them as often as she considered her own future, which was no longer set in plaster. She soaked up knowledge. She watched. She learned, biding her time and one day, she knew, she'd be free.

"Inga! My supper!" Lord Brune called from the next room.

"Yes, my lord! Coming right away," Inga called back pleasantly. She picked up the serving tray, took a breath and walked out the kitchen door.

Appendix I
Diagrams

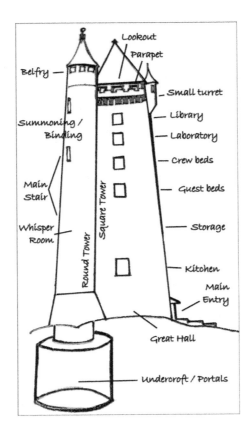

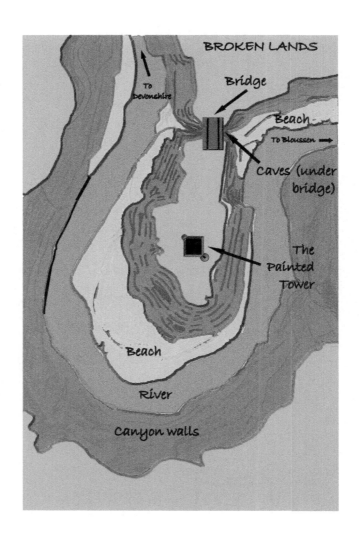

SPOILER WARNING:
Reading the following lore contained in appendices II and III before finishing the story may prematurely reveal some significant plot elements.

Appendix II
Cast of Characters

Raleigh Talanth

The second son of Hilmon Talanth and Susanna D'Normic, Raleigh stood just under six feet in height, with a slender build. He had wavy brown hair and hazel eyes. He had attained the rank of True Mage at the age of twenty, just before meeting Lana Arcana and beginning their ordeal in the storm.

Raleigh was innately curious and styled himself a seeker of the truth, the combination of which frequently landed him in difficult situations. Other magi perceived his aura as orange in color. Talanths traditionally wore maroon or rust colored robes, sometimes with red or gold accents.

Lana Arcana

Lana was a novice magi, barely out of her parent's home. Her father, Lord Desmond Arcana and her mother Trysta Pinkis held to the tradition of turning young adults out into the world to learn, hone their magic and mature before being deemed worthy of inheritance or position in the family.

Lana was just seventeen years of age when she was rescued by Raleigh from a flooded mud pit in the broken lands.

She was petite and thin with pale skin, long blonde hair and blue eyes. Her aura was a pale yellow. Arcanas were known to wear black robes. Some sects of the clan trim their black robes with silver, but Lana's were purely jet black.

Reginald Partha (Reg)

Young Reginald Partha was an apprentice to Vardan Talanth and responsible for menial tasks around the Painted Tower.

His father, Lord Perin Partha believed it wiser (and safer) to send children out into the world with some structure to further their growth and learning. It was also an emerging notion to place children with members of clans with a history of strife with one's own, in hopes of preserving peace and creating a more unified future Empire. The Talanths and the Parthas had a long animosity that Lord Perin hoped could begin to be quelled by having his son tutored in the Talanth's Painted Tower.

Reg was an amiable and dutiful young mage who had not quite attained sufficient ability for the Test of the True Mage, but was close at the time Raleigh and Lana arrived at the tower.

He was tall and thin with short, dark hair and a clean-shaven, boyish face. His aura was an orangish-yellow. Clan Partha wore red robes.

Davis Talanth

Davis was a chubby, old, gray-haired man with a no-nonsense disposition. He was on the shorter side at just five and a half feet tall. He was a widower, given charge of the Painted Tower by his clan's chieftain after Davis' much beloved wife, Darla had died. When his nephew, Vardan fell under similar, tragic circumstances, he joined Davis at the tower on an ostensibly temporary basis.

Davis was not an ambitious mage, but he didn't get to be seventy-six without learning some things. He was knowledgeable about history and fairly powerful as a magic wielder, though his skills were in decline from neglect. His aura was perceived as a burgundy color by his peers. Davis had tended the Painted Tower for over a decade before Raleigh and Lana arrived.

Vardan Talanth

Vardan had married early, but was still childless when his wife died young and unexpectedly. Distraught and directionless, he languished until the clan elders took notice of his sorry state and convinced him to move in to the Painted Tower with his uncle Davis, who was himself a widower. The idea was to give him duties to keep him occupied and at the same time, perhaps glean some helpful perspective from an older relative who'd suffered a similar loss.

They hadn't known one another before Vardan moved in to the tower, but they bonded and became very close in the years they tended the place together.

Eventually, Vardan, who was acquainted and friendly with Lord Perin Partha, agreed to take his son on as an apprentice and so Reginald Partha also moved in to the Painted Tower.

Vardan was slender and about six-feet tall with brown hair and beard. He usually wore the Maroon robes of Clan Talanth. His aura was perceived as red by his fellow magi.

Gavin DeVon

Poor Gavin was a sickly sight who never quite found his place in the world, though he tried. His ambition was high, his goals often just shy of his reach.

Born a Trueblood, he forsook his clan after he'd been passed over for a major inheritance he believed should have been his.

When Lord Alaric DeVon heard about the defection, he offered to take Gavin in as one of his own sons and so The disgruntled, orange-robed Trueblood became a brown-robed DeVon.

Gavin increased in power, wealth and authority under his adopted father's guidance, until he stumbled upon some of Alaric's dark secrets. His health rapidly declined and he seemed to age rapidly after that, but even after (because of trauma or some supernatural effect or both), he lost his ability to access magic, his ambition remained.

Gavin determined to depose Lord Alaric and become the new chieftain of Clan Devon. In pursuit of that mission, he and his adopted Brother Brune and their commoner servant girls arrived by unhappy circumstance at the Painted Tower.

Gavin looked much older than his natural sixty years. He had long gray hair that was thinning, pale, rheumy eyes and sallow skin. He wore the brown robes of his adopted clan, DeVon. After losing his magic, Gavin also lost his aura. Before that other magi would have said his aura appeared as lavender.

Brune DeVon

Brune was Gavin's younger adopted brother. Like Gavin, Brune wasn't born a DeVon, but was exiled from Clan Fiend for reasons he's never discussed, and later adopted by Lord Alaric.

Highly intelligent and adept at magic, Brune proved to be a valuable asset to Alaric's business ventures as well as his alchemical studies.

Brune had short dark hair, a muscular build, prominent jaw and intense, blazing blue eyes. He was forced to give up the white robes of Clan Fiend for the brown of Clan DeVon. Brune's aura was perceived as fairly powerful purple by other magi who were able to see it.

Inga

Inga was a young peasant girl, sixteen with dark hair and eyes. She was new to working in the DeVon household, when they landed on the beach in the canyon beneath the Painted Tower.

Inga's father, a commoner from the region of Devonshire, was gifted in his trade working leather. Because of his valued skill, he was brought into Devonshire to work in Lord Alaric DeVon's book bindery, tooling, stitching and engraving leather covers.

That position enabled him to seek favor for his daughter who was eventually brought into the DeVon household as a personal servant to Alaric's son, Brune.

Tanya

Tanya was twenty-five, strong, smart and a faithful commoner servant of the Devon household. She had a brown head of tight curls and freckles. She was designated as Gavin DeVon's personal servant. She grew up in Devonshire because her mother had also served the DeVon family, but she had died some years ago under mysterious, unexplained circumstances.

Tanya was quite adept at serving her mage lords.

Apendix III:
From the Tomes

About the Painted Tower

The Painted Tower was generally thought of as lookout tower over uncontrolled lands that abut the Empire. It was on the border between territories long controlled by clan Talanth and dangerous wildlands.

More importantly, but less known, it guarded a convergence of nodes. Three magic force lines crossed at roughly the tower's location and there was a boundary between the physical world and certain parallel elemental planes called the Three Realms. These were the supernatural, parallel worlds of wind (or air), land (or earth) and sea (or water).

Within the tower's undercroft, there were three portals, through-which a true mage with willful intent could pass into one of those other realms.

The tower itself also existed in those other planes (more precisely, a translucent, magical barrier in the shape of the tower did).

The tower's magic and its portals were originally meant to moderate passage one way or the other – to prevent unsanctioned mortals straying into the other planes and to keep elemental forces from running amok – as in the case of Grashnuk's rebellion in exile – in the mortal realm.

The portals were protected by powerful spells meant to prevent passage into the material plane by elementals, but the area around it had weakened and the Painted Tower itself was never completed.

The portals beneath the Painted Tower and the convergence of force lines in the vicinity provided a tremendous amount of magical energies to the tower which could be tapped by skilled magi.

The Whisper Room had been thought by Davis Talanth to be a rather limited and ancient communication device that could unreliably contact the Highmage directly through the ether. Since the tower is one of the few Empire assets that predates and survived the schism, it wasn't well understood or utilized, however. The Whisper Room was significantly more important than Davis ever realized.

At its inception, it could be used to contact a myriad of other outposts that were part of the Old Alliance of magi clans, but its true purpose was even larger than that.

It was actually the nerve center of the entire Painted Tower. All of its magics were accessed and directed from there, by placement of a combination of metal rods into the right receptacles, and pouring water or certain oils into the basins.

The entire tower and all of its seemingly distinct abilities were actually the same magical contrivance. The Whisper Room could open and close the portals in the undercroft, for example, but it could also enable the portal to be bypassed entirely, allowing unhindered movement of elemental creatures into the mortal plane. That was the power Grashnuk was ultimately after.

The Cathedral of Fire

As Raleigh noted, the Painted Tower's existence on other planes is reminiscent of the Cathedral of Fire, which touched the plane of elemental fire. That legendary structure seemed to burn eternally in a place called the Valley of the Battle, but the physical structure no longer existed in the realm of men. It was destroyed in a mighty magical battle in the distant past.

All that remained was the magical barrier between the former cathedral and the elemental plane of fire it abuts. That barrier merely reflects the otherworldly environment it borders.

For the same reasons, when Raleigh entered the sky realm, he saw the extra-planar projection of the tower there as reflection of the storm raging outside it in his own world.

Ranuis Talanth

Known as the founder of Clan Talanth and remembered as the greatest artificer of all time. His claim to fame was in crafting ingenious and powerful magic items that he called his "contrivances."

Ranius was one of the founders of mage society as it was known. He was one of the original thirteen magi who formed an alliance and sought to increase their collective power as well as the power of their progeny by bargaining with magical beings from other planes of existence.

The so-called "power pacts" brought the magi new powers but some came with a terrible price. Hundreds of generations later, unwitting magi were still paying for the power their distant ancestors bartered for.

Ranius Talanth, among numerous other astounding feats, was the architect of the Painted Tower and the first to enter into treaties with the king of elemental winds in the sky realm.

Ouranos, king of the winds saw a part of the tower that Ranius was designing as a potential threat to his kind and so, he entreated Ranius not to add that final piece to his great work. Ranius bartered the enchanted iron rod that was to be the Painted Tower's finial to Ouranos in exchange for access to the special magic of the wind elementals.

Morticon and Bloussen

At the first founding of the Great Mage Empire, its capitol was situated on the west coast. The land there was verdant, the climate steady and pleasant but the Schism led to such devastation that nothing could grow there anymore. The wasteland became known as the Desert of the Dead and hundreds of thousands were buried beneath or were reduced to ashes that mingled with its sandy soil.

The old capitol, called Morticon was a marvel of magic and architecture. It was said to have sunk beneath the sands, but may have just been reduced to ash and rubble, itself.

With the entire region rendered inhospitable, the Magi eventually moved their capitol city eastward and founded Bloussen near the southern coast. There, the Highmage presided over a council of the various clans' chieftains to settle disputes, enact laws and preserve the peace between the clans.

About the Author

Dan McGrath is a survivor of narcissistic abuse and recovering codependent. He's now training to become a pilot and enjoying creative hobbies like painting, writing and music production.

He has extensive experience working in and around politics and government. He has served as executive director, president and communications director for non-profit organizations, a campaign manager for candidates, chairman of a ballot committee and a registered lobbyist. He has also launched several successful lawsuits against government entities and won cases in both the Minnesota and United States Supreme Courts.

Dan has been featured in numerous national and local television and radio programs and newspapers.

Before getting roped into political work, Dan was an avid gamer, co-owner of a game and comic book shop called Red Dragon Hobby and the creator of the original 1997 role playing game, MagiQuest.

Learn more at DanMcGrath.net

Other Books by Dan McGrath

MagiQuest

What Everyone Should Know About the Government

The Adventures of Dan and Tina

The Voter Fraud Manual

Crossword Therapy

Printed in Great Britain
by Amazon

20852261R00109